MURDER
A LA
CARTE

The 4th Nikki Hunter Mystery

Nancy Skopin

Murder A La Carte
The Fourth Nikki Hunter Mystery
Copyright © 2015 by Nancy Skopin
All rights reserved.
First Print Edition: December 2015

Cover and Formatting: Streetlight Graphics

This is a work of fiction. Names, characters, places, and incidents either are the product of the author's imagination or are used fictitiously, and any resemblance to locales, events, business establishments, or actual persons—living or dead—is entirely coincidental.

In memory of Jack V. Trusty

PROLOGUE

HUGO ZOGG LOVED CHILDREN. HE'D devoted eleven years of his life to becoming a pediatrician so he could spend his days with them. He'd also spent countless hours molesting and abusing them. He had lost his own innocence to his alcoholic father when he was three.

Not a picky man, Zogg molested both boys and girls, up to the age of four. He'd discovered early in his career that children over four tended to ask questions, like, "Mommy, why did the doctor touch me like that?" He'd almost lost his license because of one precocious little boy who didn't like the way Zogg had "touched" him. The North Carolina Medical Review Board eventually ruled in his favor, determining that handling the child's genitals had been part of a routine examination. The

1

boy's parents had unsuccessfully petitioned the DA to pursue the matter. Failing that, they had then filed a civil suit, but the case was dismissed by the judge for lack of evidence. Children make lousy witnesses. Still, the review process had taken almost a year and the local newspaper had ruined Zogg's reputation. He had eventually moved to a new state to start over again. Now he was more careful.

Zogg reestablished himself in San Mateo, California. He liked California. The weather suited him and he relished the feeling of a fresh start on a different coast. He'd purchased a condo near the medical arts building where he rented an office suite. Most days he walked to work. There was a grade school along the way and he would stop to watch the kindergarteners on the playground.

He was doing just that one bright November morning when Nina Jezek walked up behind him and slipped a razor-sharp stiletto into his back. She inserted the blade below Zogg's ribcage and leaned into it, pushing it up into his heart. All he felt at first was the pressure, then he felt a stinging pain and an overwhelming chill before he sank into darkness. His lifeless body fell against the fence, his fingers still clinging to the chain link, unwilling to let go, his blind eyes fixed on the children only a few yards away.

After an hour the principal called the police, unaware that Zogg was dead, but concerned about how long he'd been standing at the playground fence.

By the time Zogg's body was discovered Nina was at home enjoying a cup of herbal tea and watching the news. She waited patiently for the breaking story about the murder of a local pediatrician. Channel 36 had sent a camera crew, which arrived while the crime scene investigation was still taking place. They hadn't moved the body yet.

Nina drank it in, knowing that if she didn't tell anyone, they would never know why he had been killed. But it didn't matter. She knew why. Zogg had been a monster. They were everywhere. One out of three little girls and one out of five little boys were reported to have been molested before the age of seven. Reported! She knew firsthand that most children who were molested never spoke with an adult about it, but carried the guilty secret inside them. No one had to tell her these crimes were usually committed by someone the child knew well—a relative, a neighbor, a babysitter, or a family friend—and that threats were often used to ensure silence.

Sometimes, as with Zogg, the predator took advantage of his position to prey on children. She'd read about him, even gone to his office to get a look at him. His eyes glowed when he gazed at the children in his waiting room. Nina had honed her instincts until they were like radar. She could spot a pedophile from ten yards away now. When she got closer, she could smell them. She could smell Zogg.

Once she'd seen him she knew he was out of control. He was a doctor. Children were entrusted to his care. Zogg was a pro at managing his obsession. Even if a parent was in the room while he was "examining" his innocent victims, they might not see what was happening or understand it if they did. Nina thought of her own mother. When the memories of what her father had done to her began to surface in her late twenties she'd considered discussing it with her mother, but she knew it would be useless. The woman lived in a world of religious denial. Nina spent as little time with her as possible, and decided it wouldn't do any good to bring it up. What would she say after so much time had passed? "Mom, why didn't you protect me?" There was no point.

Nina had followed Zogg for a week before striking. Now she sat back, feeling satisfied.

When the news report was over she turned off the TV and went to bed. She wanted to be fresh for work tonight. She had more research to do.

CHAPTER 1

M Y NAME IS NICOLI HUNTER. I'm
a private investigator working out
of a marina complex in Redwood City,
California. I became a PI because I need to
be in control of my own destiny, because I'm
compelled to see that justice is done, and
because I'm very good at spotting dishonesty
in others. I developed this skill early in life.

I'm thirty-six years old, divorced three
times, childless but not dogless, and living
aboard a 46-foot Cheoy Lee Motorsailer.
I lease a ground floor office in the marina
where my boat is docked.

Most of my business comes from the
restaurant and bar industry. I evaluate
cuisine, ambiance and, above all, employee
performance and honesty. I also participate
in exit interviews when I catch an employee

stealing from one of my clients and they need to be terminated. I do some insurance fraud investigation, occasionally monitor the activities of an unfaithful spouse, and in the last six months I've solved three cases of multiple murder.

I recently located a missing cat for my neighbor, Sarah, but that was a one-time thing. Larry, her prize-winning Persian, had been relieving himself on a neighbor's sailboat, and the boat owner had finally had enough. He'd put out several large rattraps and Larry had been snared in one of them, breaking his leg. The guy had felt guilty enough to take Larry to a local vet, but not guilty enough to tell Sarah or go back to pick him up. Once I'd scoured the marina and checked with the local shelters, I called around to the local vets until I found the right one. Animal control had a long talk with the perturbed boat owner about his traps, and he has since removed them, but I don't think Larry will be visiting his boat again any time soon.

In the years since I got my PI license I've accepted only a handful of cases that made the hair on the back of my neck bristle. I could tell the boy standing in my office doorway was going to be one of them. He appeared to be seven or eight years old. His hair was mousy-brown and falling into his eyes. He was slim, but his face was round and had a scattering of freckles. He wore a pair of tired-looking blue jeans, dirty sneakers, and a blue and red striped sweatshirt.

As he stood staring at me, he looked frightened. Most people don't find my appearance intimidating. I'm five-seven and a hundred and thirty-six pounds. I have long, curly, chestnut brown hair, and sea-blue eyes with black rims around the irises, which I inherited from my dad. Today I was dressed in jeans, a navy quarter zip sweatshirt, and New Balance cross trainers. Just like him. See, not intimidating.

I am not good with kids. I had a miserable childhood and I don't like to be reminded of it. Spending time in the company of children takes me back, particularly if the child in question is unhappy. The boy in the doorway continued staring at me for about a minute, and I reluctantly returned his gaze. Eye contact of this type is almost preternatural. Eventually I felt something between the two of us clunk into place.

After the clunk thing happened, he said, "Are you Hunter?"

The sign on my office door, and in all my ads, reads 'Hunter Investigations'.

"I am," I said. "What can I do for you?"

I may be uncomfortable with kids, but I always try to treat them with respect. It's been my experience that children behave in a more civilized manner when you treat them like adults.

"I want you to find out who killed my mom," he said.

He stuck out his chin when he said this, as though daring me to turn him away. I rarely turn anyone away before at least having a conversation with them.

"You want to sit down?" I asked.

He remained in the doorway, surveying the office. I had the impression he was checking to make sure it was safe to come inside. When his eyes reached my desk they lowered, landing on Buddy, my dog, who was watching complacently from his spot on the floor next to my chair. Buddy is an eighty-five pound cross between a Rhodesian Ridgeback and a Golden Retriever. He's about seven months old and is steadily gaining height, weight, and muscle.

As the boy approached my desk Buddy took more of an interest. This was a small intruder, but Buddy tends to put himself between me and any stranger who gets too close. He drew himself up from his resting place and stretched slowly, then moved around the side of the desk and inserted himself between me and my guest.

"I hope you're not afraid of dogs," I said. He looked at Buddy apprehensively. "He's friendly," I added.

He never took his eyes off Buddy, but appeared to have heard me, because he reached out a tentative hand. Buddy stepped closer, sniffed the proffered hand, licked it once, and allowed the boy to pet him. After this little ritual had been observed the boy sat down in one of my visitor's chairs with Buddy at his feet. I opened a drawer to take out a legal pad and saw him flinch at the movement. He was exhibiting symptoms of hypervigilance. He'd probably either been beaten or verbally abused at some point in his life. I held up the legal pad so he could see it wasn't a weapon, set it on my blotter, and picked up a ballpoint pen.

We looked at each other some more and eventually he spoke. "She was murdered." I wrote that down, assuming he was still talking about his mom. "What are you writing?" he asked.

"I'm taking notes," I said. "Sometimes I

forget things, so I write everything down." I tried a smile, but he wasn't having any.

"What's your name?" I asked.

"Why do you need to know that?"

"If you want me to work for you I need to know your name."

"So, you'll take the case?" he asked.

"I don't know yet. I need more information about what happened, and you have to be completely honest with me. No hiding stuff because you don't think I need to know."

He appeared to be mulling that over. "I'll tell you what happened," he said.

It was a short story. He and his mother had been shopping at Mervyn's in Redwood City on a Saturday, two weeks ago. He'd outgrown his jeans. His mom was in the fitting room with him, which he found totally embarrassing. He didn't actually say that. I guessed it by the way his face colored when he told that part of the story. His mom had gone to get him another size and she'd never come back. He'd waited a long time, then put his own clothes back on and went looking for her.

When he came out of the fitting room several people were gathered by the wall of boys' jeans. He'd pushed his way through,

Nancy Skopin

knowing something was wrong. When he reached the center of the crowd he saw his mom lying on the floor. She was on her back, he said, and her eyes were open. He could tell she was dead. He'd knelt beside her and felt for a pulse like he'd seen people do on TV. One of the adults had tried to pull him away and he'd punched the guy in the chest and shouted, *"Get off me. She's my mom."*

Interesting choice of words, I thought. "Then what happened?" I asked.

"The paramedics came and tried to help her, but it was too late. They covered her up and the police made everybody move back. Some people wearing uniforms came and did things to her, and took some pictures. Then they took her away. The police said I had to go with them. They took me to the station and put me in a room. A man came in and asked me what happened. He was nice, so I told him. Then a lady came and talked to me about my family. She wanted to know about my dad. I told her I didn't have a dad and she left me alone for a long time. Then my aunt came and got me. I live with her now, but she doesn't like me. My mom and her didn't get along."

The whole time he was talking to me he was petting Buddy. Dogs are first-rate tranquilizers.

12

"Aren't you supposed to be in school today?" I asked. He looked startled, like I might be trying to trap him. "It's okay," I said, holding up my hands in a gesture of surrender. "I used to cut school all the time. I was just wondering."

"Yeah, I'm supposed to be in school. The thing is, the police won't tell me what happened to my mom, and it's not right. It's just not right," he whispered.

I wondered what wasn't right. That the police wouldn't talk to a child about his mother's murder, that she had been murdered in the first place, or the fact that he had to live with his aunt who didn't like him. I was feeling sorry for the kid and that usually spells trouble for me.

"What do you want me to do?" I asked.

"I want you to find out who did it," he said. "I can pay you. At least I think I can. My mom had life insurance. I'm supposed to get some money."

He was too young to know how life insurance worked. If the aunt was his legal guardian, she would probably have control of any inheritance.

I put down my pen and folded my hands over the legal pad. "If you want me to investigate your mom's death, you have to answer a few more questions for me. You and I will sign a contract, and then I'll talk to the police and see what I can find out. Okay?"

"Okay."

"Let's start with your name and date of birth."

Date of birth would probably be easier for him to respond to than age. Age might imply that he was too young to be doing what he was doing. Of course he *was* too young to be doing this, but I wasn't going to be the one to tell him that.

"Scott Freedman," he said. "October twenty-first." He hesitated a moment and then told me the year.

I wrote down the information. My new client was nine years old. That meant he was in the third grade. He was small for his age.

"What was your mom's name?" I asked.

"Gloria Freedman," he said.

"What's not right?" I asked, looking him in the eye.

"Huh?"

"Before, you said 'it's just not right.' What did you mean?"

His eyes fogged over for an instant and then cleared as he evidently remembered what he had said. "What happened to my mom. It's not right for people to kill each other like animals."

I wondered where he'd heard that phrase.

"How do you know your mom was killed? Maybe she had a heart attack or something."

"I saw the blood," he said.

"What's your phone number, Scott?" I asked.

He thought about that some and then picked up a business card from the dish on my desk. "Can I call you?"

"Sure. You can do that. But what if I have more questions?"

"My aunt's weird about the telephone," he said.

"Okay. No problem. You can call me collect if you want."

I turned to my computer and pulled up my standard contract, entered Scott's name and the date, and the sum of $5.00 as a deposit against services to be rendered. Of course, as a legal technicality contracts with minors are invalid, but I'd honor it just the same.

"Do you have five dollars?" I asked, as I printed the form.

Scott reached into his jeans pocket and came up with some change.

"Close enough," I said.

We both signed the contract and I asked Scott if he wanted a copy.

"Yes, please," he said.

Considering all he had been through, Scott was extremely composed. I may not know much about children, but I study psychology in my spare time and I could tell that something in Scott's life had caused him to mature beyond his years.

"Call me before school tomorrow," I said.

"Okay."

He rose from his chair and walked toward the door, studying his copy of the contract as he went. When he reached the door he turned back to me. "Thank you, Hunter," he said. There were tears in his eyes. He turned away quickly and I resisted the urge to follow and make sure he got where he was going safely. It was chillier than usual for December on the California coast, but at least it wasn't raining. He'd probably be fine.

CHAPTER 2

A FTER SCOTT LEFT, BUDDY LOOKED across the desk at me as if to say, "What are you going to do about this?" Sometimes I imagine he has human characteristics. I looked back into his big chocolate-brown eyes and said, "I'll take care of it." He tilted his head to one side while I called Bill Anderson.

Bill and I have been dating since last July, when the mother of a young woman who was brutally murdered hired me to investigate because she was unhappy with the local homicide dicks. Bill was one of the dicks in question. He's thirty-seven and just under six feet tall, slim but muscular, and has a brilliant smile, black hair, and hazel eyes. He has some issues with the way I work, but that's pretty much the only thing we argue about. Two months ago Bill suggested we try living together. I vetoed that idea, unwilling to give up my freedom and privacy to that extent; however his occasional overnight visits are just fine with me.

The phone rang once before he picked up.

"Anderson," he said in a gruff voice.

"Tough day?" I asked.

"Hi, Nikki."

My heart warmed at the change in his tone of voice once he knew it was me. I'm pretty crazy about Bill. Most of the time when I'm with him I feel like life is full of hope and promise. Unfortunately, feeling hopeful scares the crap out of me.

"I have a new case," I said. "Gloria Freedman's son just left my office."

"Scottie?"

"Yeah. How old is he?" I wasn't convinced Scott had been honest about his date of birth.

"He's nine, but he's small for his age. He should be in school, damn it."

"His mom is dead. Maybe he doesn't feel like going to school. What can you tell me?"

"Nothing, right now. I'll talk to you tonight."

Bill works in a bullpen-type environment with a bunch of other detectives and can't always talk about an ongoing investigation with me, or anyone else who isn't in law enforcement. Knowing this doesn't stop me from asking.

"What would you like for dinner?" I asked.

"Is this a domestic bribe?"

"Absolutely."

"In that case, I'd like a large Hawaiian pizza and a nice bottle of Cabernet."

"How late are you working tonight?"

"I'll probably get off around six."

"I'll see you then. I have to do a survey in San Francisco later tonight. Would you mind Buddy sitting?"

"That shouldn't be a problem."

We said goodbye after muttering the usual endearments that I know Bill finds embarrassing. Serves him right for being such a guy.

Buddy was still watching me when I hung up the phone.

"That was Bill," I said.

Of course, he already knew that. Buddy has extrasensory hearing. He can hear Bill's Mustang when it exits the freeway almost a mile from the marina. His ears perk up and he starts running laps around the office until I hook his leash to his collar and walk him out to the parking lot. The same thing happens when we're aboard the boat, except instead of running laps he just lets himself out of the hatch and stands in the pilothouse waiting for me to open the door.

I made a quick call to my best friend, Elizabeth, and invited her along for the San Francisco job. The restaurant I needed to survey tonight was one of her favorites because it's often filled with celebrities. Elizabeth lives aboard a trawler not far from where my sailboat is docked. She enthusiastically agreed to accompany me to the city, and I told her I'd pick her up at 7:30.

After we ended the call I decided to visit Mervyn's to see if anyone wanted to gossip about the recent murder.

I drive a vintage 1972 British racing green BMW model 2002. Since I adopted Buddy the backseat is carpeted with short, red dog hair. When we arrived at Mervyn's I parked in a shady spot and opened the windows enough so Buddy would have fresh air, but not enough for him to escape. I told him I wouldn't be long. I always say that when I leave him in the car and he never believes me.

CHAPTER 3

I ENTERED THE MERVYN'S STORE AND found my way to the boyswear department, located the wall of jeans, and turned to find the fitting room about twenty feet away. The cashier was a young Hispanic woman whose nametag read Giselle. At the moment she was on the phone, speaking rapidly in Spanish. I approached the counter and took out my PI license.

Sometimes I pretend to be something I'm not, and sometimes I just cut to the chase and ask for information. At the moment I didn't feel like pretending, so when Giselle hung up the phone, I presented her with my license and a business card, and asked if she had a minute to speak with me.

"Am I in trouble?"

"Not that I know of," I said, smiling.

"I'm handling an investigation for the family of the woman who was killed here."

Giselle looked around the store, perhaps concerned someone might overhear. She was in her mid-twenties, five-six, with long dark hair pulled back in a ponytail. She was dressed in beige slacks and a purple sweater, and she was pretty, but I had the impression she was short on self-confidence.

"Were you working that day?" I asked.

"No," she said. "It was a Saturday. I work Sunday through Friday, but I was here to have lunch with Essie, my sister. Essie works Saturdays." She flushed and her eyes darted around the store again. "Please don't tell anyone," she whispered. "They don't know we're sisters. If they find out we could lose our jobs."

Many retail organizations have anti-nepotism policies because working with a relative encourages collaborative shoplifting and till-tapping. I know this because I worked in retail security management when I was in my twenties.

"I won't say a word," I said. "I'm only interested in what happened to the woman who was killed."

"I didn't see anything."

She paused, and I thought maybe that

was it. I waited silently, hoping for more. Finally she took another furtive look around and leaned across the counter.

"Essie heard the woman yelling at her kid in the fitting room. She said it was terrible. That poor little boy. She was in there with him while he was trying on jeans, Essie said, and she kept yelling at him to hurry up 'cause she had better things to do. She even said she wished he'd never been born. Can you believe that? Some people shouldn't have kids."

I agreed with her. In my opinion, people should be required to go through a training program and a psychological screening process before becoming parents.

"Did Essie say anything else?"

"No. Just that the kid was quiet, like he was used to getting yelled at."

So, Scott was a victim. Interesting that he loved his mom in spite of her treatment of him. Some kids will take the abuse and love you anyway. Scott would have to make some difficult choices in the years to come. Most children who suffer physical or psychological abuse become either bullies or chronic victims. I couldn't help wondering which direction Scott would choose.

My own childhood was not without

trauma. My cousin Aaron used to misbehave when no one was watching and then point his finger at me, convincing my parents that I was the one who was guilty of his crimes. I received frequent spankings and was sent to my room without TV privileges more times that I can count. I hated Aaron as a child, but now we're sort of on speaking terms. He's a criminal defense attorney and, not surprisingly, excels in his chosen field. My other childhood issues revolve around the fact that my mother is a former nun and my dad was born a Cossack.

Giselle volunteered to ask Essie if she remembered anything else that might help me. I gave her another of my business cards for her sister, thanked her for her time, and left.

When I got back to the parking lot it looked as though Buddy hadn't moved since I'd entered the store. His nose was pressed against the window and he had been watching the door he'd seen me go in through.

"I came back again," I said, as I unlocked the car.

He sighed heavily and curled up on the back seat.

CHAPTER 4

NINA JEZEK WORKED A SWING *shift data entry job and attempted to sleep during the day. The dreams didn't bother her so much now that she knew they were actually memories. She had started having them a few weeks after her twenty-seventh birthday, which was the night her father had killed himself. She'd come home to visit her mom for a week, but had been staying at the Holiday Inn rather than with her parents.*

Her father had invited her over for dinner, but she'd told him she had other plans. Her mother had been at a club event that night, so her father was alone. He'd been ill for some time, but had outlived every prediction his doctors had made. He probably would have lived another ten or fifteen years. She'd never

Nancy Skopin

know what might have happened if she had accepted his dinner invitation.

The last eight years of his life Nina had been living in D.C., but she would call every couple of weeks, and made a point of talking with her dad each time. It hadn't been easy. Her father had been Czech and, even with all the years he'd been in the states, there was still a language barrier, which put even more distance between them. For reasons she hadn't understood at the time, Nina had grown up fearing that her father would kill her.

She didn't really have plans the night he took his own life, but it was her birthday, and she didn't want to be around him on her birthday. When she received the phone call from her mother the next day, she'd felt guilty and ashamed. Then the dreams began and a different kind of shame had surfaced.

Nina had gone to a couple of psychiatrists, and each of them had diagnosed her with post traumatic stress disorder and recommended pharmaceutical therapy. When she'd told one of them about her dreams, the woman had explained that the mind often replays events we're unable to deal with as dreams. The anxiety worsened, initially, when she realized they weren't dreams at all, but memories.

At first she felt responsible for what her

father had done to her. She felt unclean, disgusted, and damaged. She hadn't dated anyone since. But along with the shame, Nina had also experienced a profound sense of relief. She finally understood why sexual predators were drawn to her. She had been kidnapped and gang-raped when she was fifteen and molested by three physicians during her teen years: an oral surgeon, a podiatrist, and an OBGYN. She was thirty now, and only went to female doctors.

Nina's father had begun fondling her when she was six months old. When she was old enough to talk he had choked her while molesting her, threatening to kill her if she told anyone. She had run away from home for the first time at the age of three, believing her survival depended on getting away from her family. The molestation had continued until she was five, when she started kindergarten.

She had repressed the horror so completely that she was incapable of remembering the assaults until her father was dead and no longer a threat. That's when the memories had returned as dreams.

CHAPTER 5

By 6:00 I had the Hawaiian pizza box wrapped in heavy-duty aluminum foil to keep it warm, the cabernet uncorked, and a glass poured for Bill so it could breathe. I was wearing nothing but a short black chemise. I take bribing public officials very seriously.

One of many changes in my life since Bill and I started dating is the acquisition of some sexy lingerie. I thought it might be nice for him to see me in something other than jeans or shorts, my usual work uniform, and I was right. The first time I'd surprised him with a garter belt and stockings his eyes had widened and his trousers had grown snug. I liked that reaction, so I purchased a few more items, among them the chemise.

At 6:03 Buddy bounded up the companionway, took the leather pull-cord in his mouth, cranked it to the left, and pushed outward with his nose opening the hatch. He lunged into the pilothouse, but I had intentionally closed the pilothouse door so he couldn't get out on deck. I watched as he head butted the door and then turned to gaze down at me.

"You can wait," I said. "He'll be here in a minute."

He tilted his head to one side and whined. Buddy is a quiet dog; rambunctious and energetic, but quiet. Now he started mewing and chuffing, making sounds that were so close to words I could hardly stand it. When I didn't come up the steps and open the door for him, he lifted a paw and scratched at the door a couple of times, then opened his mouth and took the handle between his teeth.

"Hey!" I shouted. "What are you doing?"

I should have known. He'd seen me open that door dozens of times and it had only taken him one try to get the more complicated hatch open. Moments later he was out on deck.

"Buddy, stay!" I yelled. *"Shit,"* I said more quietly.

Normally Buddy waits for me to join him with the leash and we walk up to the parking lot together to meet Bill. Today, however, I was not dressed, and I wondered how long he would wait before making the journey on his own. I pulled on a pair of jeans, quickly tucking the chemise in, and felt the boat rock as Buddy jumped onto the dock. I should have locked the damn door.

"Buddy, stay!"

I stepped into my boat shoes and grabbed a jacket before running down the dock after him.

He was waiting at the gate when I arrived. I'd forgotten to grab his leash so I hooked my fingers under his collar.

"Bad dog," I whispered.

He looked up at me, his tail wagging frantically. I'd also forgotten my gate key and I felt exposed, being commando under the jeans and jacket I'd hastily pulled on over the chemise.

Bill drove into the parking lot and I pushed open the gate. Buddy dragged me along as he loped toward the Mustang.

"Slow *down*," I shouted.

Bill was out of his car and laughing when we reached him.

"This is not *funny*," I said, as Buddy jumped up and licked his face. "Your dog has a discipline problem."

"My dog? Now he's my dog?"

"Only when he misbehaves."

"Of course," he said, and ruffled Buddy's ears.

"I wasn't dressed, so I thought we'd wait for you on the boat tonight. He opened the hatch and the pilothouse door all by himself and went out on deck. I told him to stay, but he didn't, so I had to get dressed and chase after him."

"Have you trained him to stay?"

"I've tried."

Bill turned his attention away from the affectionate canine and regarded me. "You weren't dressed?"

"I wasn't dressed *and* he left the boat without me," I repeated. His smile grew. "I had plans," I said, blushing. "But I may not be in the mood anymore."

"Bad dog," Bill said. He threw an arm around me and took hold of Buddy's collar. "We'll work on doggie discipline later tonight," he said, and he kissed me.

The kiss put me back in the mood. I forgot about the discipline problem and my thoughts returned to my previous designs for the evening. Sex, pizza and wine for Bill, and talk about Scott's case—in that order, then a trip to the city with my best friend.

While Bill was eating we offered Buddy pizza toppings if he would sit and stay for a full minute. This seemed to work pretty well as long as there was a reward being offered, but when we told him to stay and didn't offer a treat, the results varied.

"So tell me about Scott's mom," I said, tossing Buddy a chunk of pineapple.

Bill took a sip of his wine. "You know I'm not supposed to discuss ongoing investigations." I said nothing. He always feels the need to remind me of this. "Her throat was abraded as though someone had grabbed hold of her windpipe so she couldn't cry out. She was stabbed with a long narrow double-edged blade—upward through the diaphragm and into the heart. My guess is that she was looking into the eyes of her killer when she died. There was garlic in the wound. Garlic keeps blood from coagulating."

"Yikes," I said.

"Yeah. What's really frightening is that the store was crowded at the time, and nobody saw anything."

"How is that even possible?" I asked.

"People avoid looking at each other in public places. Do you ever look at other people when you're shopping?"

"Sometimes when I'm waiting in line and I have nothing else to do. But the people who look back at me almost always look away again."

"Exactly. Contact with people we don't know is threatening. And what if the person you're looking at is unbalanced? With the increase in population, dementia is on the rise. Plus, with all the recent terrorist activity, people feel more defensive than ever."

He was right about the population thing. I'd read about a study done with rats that allowed them to reproduce until their cage became crowded. When it got so crowded that movement was restricted the adult males began sexually assaulting the young, and killing and eating them along with the weaker adults. Of course human beings are not rodents, most of the time.

"Any similar homicides in other jurisdictions?" I asked.

"I'm still working on that sex offender case from last month. Remember I told you about the pedophile who was murdered near the daycare center on Middlefield?" I nodded. "He was killed with the same type of weapon. Long, narrow, very sharp, also coated with garlic." He looked at me.

"You're not going to bother any other police departments with this case are you?"

"Why would I do that when I can get all the information I need from you?" I gave him an innocent smile and batted my eyelashes.

He chuckled. "I mean it, Nikki. I'll tell you what I know if you promise not to bother anyone else."

"I promise." I saluted.

"There are two other homicides that might be related. A pediatrician named Hugo Zogg was stabbed outside a schoolyard in San Mateo, and a known sex offender named Juan Fernandez was killed in Sunnyvale two days after he was released from Lompoc. In both cases the weapon was a knife with a long narrow blade and there was garlic in the wound."

I felt my mouth drop open. "Oh my God," I said. I grabbed a pad and started taking notes.

"Don't jump to conclusions."

I looked at him. "Did you do a background check on the pediatrician?"

"It's not my case," he said.

"Did the San Mateo PD run a background on the pediatrician?"

He nodded. "There were charges filed against him two years ago by the parents of a boy in North Carolina. The medical review board found in the doctor's favor. The parents filed a civil suit and went to the local newspaper, and eventually the doctor moved to California."

"Molestation charges?" I asked.

"Yeah."

I remembered what Giselle had told me about Scott's mother. "Did you talk to the cashiers at Mervyn's?"

"Of course."

"So did I."

"There's no evidence that Scottie's mother abused him."

"That depends on your definition of abuse. If the killer is some kind of vigilante avenging abused children it might not matter what kind of abuse we're talking about. Sexual, emotional, or psychological. Did you interview Scott?"

"Yes, but he was pretty shaken up at the time."

"And you didn't know about the weapon yet."

"No, I didn't."

"So you probably didn't ask him about the way his mother yelled at him, or if she ever hit him when she was angry."

"Nope."

Bill looked like he was getting a little pissed off, so I didn't bother to tell him I would have that conversation with Scott.

We didn't talk any more about the case that night, but I was still thinking about it as I dressed for my dinner with Elizabeth.

CHAPTER 6

IT WAS 60 DEGREES IN Redwood City, but
I knew San Francisco would be cooler so
I pulled on a pair of knee-high black leather
boots and a snug black knit dress with a
sexy little cutout across the chest. After
scrunching my curls with gel and applying
lip gloss, I tucked the Glock into my black
pistol purse, and threw on an emerald-green
wool coat with a faux fur collar: a little
color to break up all the black. When I'd
spotted the coat on sale at Nordstrom, I'd
loved it so much that I broke my own rule
about keeping my wardrobe to a minimum
to conserve space.

Elizabeth was waiting aboard her trawler
with her door wide open, as is her custom
when it's not freezing or rainy. Elizabeth
is a pixie; just over five feet tall and about

a hundred pounds. She's thirty-four years old, has strawberry blonde hair, a dusting of freckles, hazel eyes, and dimples. Tonight she was dressed in an off white turtleneck sweater dress with a wide black belt, black tights, and black ankle boots. After giving me a quick hug she wrapped herself in a hooded charcoal-colored cape and picked up her shoulder bag.

"You look stunning," I said.

"So do you sweetie. You mentioned San Francisco. Are we going where I hope we're going?"

"Yep. Your favorite restaurant. Just try not to stare too much if you see any celebrities."

"I'll try, but I'm not making any promises."

On the way to the city I told her about Scott, and, because I knew she could keep a secret, I told her what Bill had shared with me about his mother's murder, the wound trajectory and type of knife, the three similar killings in the area and, finally, the garlic.

"Yikes!"

"That's what I said."

"So you're thinking maybe Scott's mom was abusing him?"

"It's possible. But it could also be that the killer heard Gloria yelling at Scott and the verbal abuse just pushed him, or her, over the edge."

When we arrived at the restaurant on Montgomery Street there were no parking spaces available, so I cruised around the block and parked in an underground lot. It was chilly, but the short walk would do us both good, especially after dinner.

We entered the lobby of the famous eatery and I was pleased to see that there was a new hostess at the podium. I'd had a part in that, since the former hostess had been a first-class bitch. The somewhat matronly, but impeccably dressed, woman greeted us warmly and offered to check our coats before asking if we had a reservation. She was a welcome addition to the restaurant's staff. Her predecessor had made me feel like I was imposing by asking to be seated.

I gave her my name, and she quickly checked the reservation ledger and then collected two menus and escorted us to a table. She informed us that our server tonight would be Sean, and that he would be right with us. No sooner had she returned to the podium than a lovely young man of mixed-race approached our table. He was over six feet tall, in his mid-twenties, and had a mocha-latte complexion, dark wavy hair, brown bedroom eyes, and a smile that was accentuated by a single dimple.

"My name is Sean," he said as he filled our water goblets. "Would you ladies like anything from the bar?"

Elizabeth fanned herself with her menu and practically vibrated as she said, "A tall mudslide, please, Sean."

Although she was engaged, Sean was a looker, and Elizabeth appreciates beauty wherever she finds it.

"Very good," he bowed slightly and turned to me.

"I'm tonight's designated driver," I demurred, "so how about an Irish coffee with half a shot of Jameson's?"

Sean showed me his dimple and said he'd be right back.

"Yowza," Elizabeth said as soon as he was out of earshot.

"*Seriously* hot," I replied.

Once she was no longer distracted by our waiter, Elizabeth turned her attention to the other patrons in the crowded restaurant. "Oh my *God*," she whispered. "Is that Zac Efron?"

"Um, probably?"

"And is that Sami with him? She is so adorable."

"Elizabeth. You're staring."

"Right. Sorry. Would you mind if I just took a quick photo with your smartphone?" Elizabeth refuses to own a cell phone.

"Yes, I *would* mind, and I think Zac and Sami would too."

Elizabeth pouted for only a moment before Sean returned and served our drinks. Then she refocused her attention on him, enjoying the view.

Sean recited the evening's specials, and asked if we'd like time to consider the menu. We both already knew what we wanted, and ordered the Caesar salad for two. I requested the Coulotte steak with a Bordeaux reduction sauce and morel mushrooms, and Elizabeth ordered the stuffed lamb chops.

Less than ten minutes later we were being entertained by Sean as he blended the Caesar dressing ingredients together at the table, asking if we wanted anchovies or ground pepper, and then expertly tossing the salad before serving us. This was one of my favorite restaurants, and not because of their celebrity clientele. In spite of constant dieting, I'm a bit of a foodie, and the chef and saucier at this establishment were outstanding.

Sean proved to be a very professional, attentive, charming, and as far as I could tell, honest server. His other tables never seemed to be neglected, but when my water glass was half empty, he was immediately at my side with the pitcher. Not only would this guy receive high praise in my report, but I'd tip more than usual for this kind of service.

Elizabeth and I talked about her upcoming wedding to my former client, Jack McGuire. I'd introduced them when I was working a case for Jack last August, and the two had hit it off like a house-a-fire. They were still discussing potential dates and venues, but hadn't settled on anything yet. Jack had suggested a June wedding and Elizabeth said that wouldn't give her enough time to plan, unless it was a year from next June, 18 months from now. Fine with me. I was in no hurry to see my best friend move away from the marina.

Overall it was a totally enjoyable evening and an exceptionally good survey.

When we arrived back at the marina I walked Elizabeth down to her trawler and gave her a quick squeeze.

"Thanks for coming with me tonight."

"Thanks for bringing me. Sweet dreams, honey."

I ambled down the dock, stopping briefly

to scratch behind D'Artagnon's ears before continuing on to my boat. D'Artagnon is a loveable black Lab who lives aboard a Bluewater 42 powerboat with one of my neighbors. He's an excellent watchdog. In fact, he saved my life not long ago; but even before that D'Artagnon was one of my favorite canines.

As I let myself in through the pilothouse door I heard whining. I opened the hatch and looked down at Bill who had a tight grip on Buddy's collar.

"Let me get down the companionway before you release the hound," I said.

Bill smiled and nodded. Buddy squirmed and whined some more. As soon as my feet hit the galley floor Buddy slipped out of his collar and jumped up to greet me. Hard to believe I'd resisted having a dog for three years because I didn't want to endure another loss. I knew Buddy would only be with me for twelve to fifteen years, and it would destroy me when his time was up, but it was *so* worth it.

CHAPTER 7

ON TUESDAY MORNING I WOKE up feeling guilty about last night's high calorie dinner. I needed to work out to get rid of the guilt, so I climbed into my sweats, ran my fingers through my curls, and trudged up to the parking lot with Buddy. We stopped along the way to say good morning to D'Artagnon. I scratched under his chin and behind his ears, and told him what a good boy he was. Buddy stretched up to his full height, front paws on the deck of the Bluewater, so he and D'Artagnon could touch noses.

After Buddy's morning walk, we drove to the Redwood City Athletic Center. The gym is less than a mile from the marina, so we were there in a few minutes. Buddy waited in the car. He'd be bored, but it was better than leaving him alone on the boat, and Bill had left early for work.

I did a hundred sit-ups and used the nautilus lower body equipment, then ran on the treadmill and climbed on the StairMaster. I showered in the locker room and appraised myself in the mirror while I was dressing. I'm in pretty good shape, in spite of a minor weight gain caused by the lack of nicotine in my system.

I was in my office sipping coffee with Buddy at my side by 7:30. My office is like a sanctuary to me. I rented it when I moved aboard the sailboat, right after I got my PI license and my most recent divorce. It's a corner office, so I have two walls of windows which afford me a view of the water, the picturesque grounds, and the sky. My desk is turned toward a wall without windows, so the scenery doesn't distract me when I'm trying to work.

The phone rang at 7:42, and I took a deep breath before answering. "Hunter Investigations."

A computer-generated voice said, "If you will accept a collect call from Scott, say yes now."

I said, "Yes," and then heard nothing.

I waited a beat before saying, "Scott, are you there?"

"Hi, Hunter."

"Are you at school?"

"Why?"

"No reason. I was wondering if you could come see me this afternoon. I need to ask you some more questions."

"I can come now."

"No, that's okay. Go to school and come see me after. Or I can pick you up if you want."

There was a brief pause, and then I heard him sigh. "That won't work. My aunt found out I cut yesterday, so she's picking me and my cousins up after school."

"Why don't I come and meet you at lunch time?"

"Can you bring your dog?"

I smiled. "He goes everywhere with me. What school and what time?"

"Spring Valley Elementary in Millbrae. Lunch is at twelve. You can pick me up out front."

I hung up the phone and logged onto the internet. Spring Valley Elementary was on Murchison Drive, about twenty minutes from the marina.

I typed up reports until 11:30, and then

Buddy and I took a walk before driving to Millbrae.

We arrived at the school at 11:53. With time to spare, I parked on the street and hooked Buddy to his leash. We wandered around the neighborhood for a few minutes, then I put him back in the car and leaned against the Bimmer to wait. Since Scott hadn't seen my car before, I thought it wise to make myself visible.

At 12:05 Scott exited the front doors of the school and ran down the steps. He spotted me instantly and, even from a distance, I could see he was upset.

"Get in the car," he shouted as he drew closer.

I was puzzled, but I got in the car anyway. He pulled open the passenger door, jumped in, slammed the door, and slid low in the seat. I looked down at him and then up at the front of the building, where I saw two kids who had apparently followed him outside.

"Are those your cousins?" I asked.

"Can we go, please?"

I started the car and pulled away from the curb. When we were a few blocks from the school I pulled over.

"You can sit up now. What's going on?"

"They saw me leaving," he said. "They called my name just as I was going out the door. It was too late to stop, so I ran. We're not supposed to leave the school grounds at lunchtime. They'll tell my aunt and I'll get in trouble again." There was a film of tears in his eyes.

"What happens when you get in trouble?" I asked gently.

He looked up at me and I saw the dread. If Scott's mother had been abusive with him, the odds were good her sister would exhibit the same behavior.

"Does your aunt hit you?" I asked.

Scott didn't answer immediately. He looked out the side window for a moment, then turned to the back seat and reached out a hand, which Buddy licked.

I wanted to turn on my tape recorder so I could play back the conversation for Bill later, but I remembered how paranoid Scott had been in my office.

"You want some gum?" I asked. "I'm gonna have some gum."

"Okay."

I picked up my purse, set it on my lap, and turned on the recorder before reaching into the zipper compartment where I keep the sugarless gum.

"Cinnamon okay?"

"Cinnamon's good."

"Where should we go for lunch?"

"MacDonald's?"

"Of course. What was I thinking?"

I put the car in gear and headed for El Camino Real.

"Scott," I said quietly, "you promised to answer all my questions, remember? If you want me to find out what happened to your mom, I need to know some things about your family."

"Why?"

"So I can understand the motive." I hoped he watched enough TV crime drama to grasp what I was saying.

He chewed his gum, looking out the passenger side window, and softly said, "Sometimes."

"Sometimes your aunt hits you?"

He nodded. Not much good for the tape, but if I tried to pry a verbal response out of him he might clam up.

"Where does she hit you?" I asked.

"In the garage."

I stifled a laugh.

"So your aunt takes you out to the garage, and then what does she do?"

He squirmed uncomfortably in his seat. I could tell I was losing him.

"It's important, Scott," I said. "Your aunt's behavior will tell me things about your mom, and the better I understand your mom the easier it will be for me to find the person who hurt her."

He swung around in his seat and glared at me. "They didn't *hurt* her," he shouted. "They fucking *killed* her!" He covered his face with his hands and unleashed a torrent of gut-wrenching sobs.

Buddy poked at Scott's shoulder with his nose, wanting to make it better. The poor kid had suffered so much already, and now, on top of everything else, his aunt was beating him.

"I'm sorry," I murmured.

We arrived at MacDonald's and I pulled into the drive-through lane. I ordered three Big Macs with cheese, jumbo fries, a diet soda, and a chocolate shake. I turned to Scott, who had stopped crying and was wiping his nose on his jacket sleeve.

"You want anything else?" I asked.

"Apple pie," he whispered.

"And an apple pie," I repeated.

A disembodied voice repeated my order, told me how much I owed, and asked me to pull up to the window. Buddy leaned forward between the two seats, sniffing the air. He turned his head toward Scott and gave him a sloppy kiss on the cheek. Scott wrapped his arms around Buddy's neck and hugged him. Oh, great. Now *I* was going to cry.

I paid the cashier at the window and handed Scott all the food. He promptly fed Buddy a French fry.

"I ordered him his own burger," I said, as Scott fed Buddy another fry. "Those are kind of hot. If you feed a dog food that's too hot it will burn his tongue and temporarily damage his sense of smell. Could you blow on the fries before you feed them to him?"

Scott took another fry out of the bag and blew on it a couple of times while Buddy leaned against him. When Scott pulled the fry further away, Buddy licked his face again. Scott crumbled into a fit of giggles and surrendered the fry. Canine therapy.

I found a deserted residential street and parked the car so we could talk and eat in peace. I took the Big Mac Scott handed me, unwrapped it, and peeled back the bun to get at the meat and cheese, which I fed to Buddy in small bites.

"So?" I said.

Scott took a bite of his burger and chewed slowly before responding. "Sometimes she pulls my pants down first," he said. He took another bite. I waited. "She has this yardstick. It's like a ruler, only bigger. She hits me on the butt with the yardstick."

"Hard?"

He grimaced at the memory. "Yeah," he said, "pretty hard."

"What else does she do?"

He looked up at me. "Isn't that enough?"

I wiped my hands on a napkin. "Is that everything?" I asked.

He seemed to think about the question. "She yells at me a lot."

"What kind of things does she yell?" I asked.

"You know, the usual stuff. That she wishes I was never born."

Apparently this was something both Gloria and her sister had heard growing up.

"*Jesus Christ*," I said before I could stop myself. "Sorry. You know she doesn't mean that, right?"

Scott bit into the pie, looking thoughtful. "I'm pretty sure she means it, Hunter."

"You can call me Nicoli if you want," I said. "That's my first name."

"Isn't that a boy's name?"

"Yeah. My dad wanted a son. My friends call me Nikki."

"Okay, Nikki." He smirked.

"Did your mom used to hit you when she got mad?" I pressed on. He was still grieving for his mother, but I needed to know.

He nodded and spit up some food into his napkin.

"Too hot?" I asked, offering him an out other than the obvious fact that he was gagging on the memory. "Buddy would be happy to eat that for you."

He turned to the back seat and offered the napkin full of regurgitated burger. Buddy not only ate the burger, he also wolfed down half the napkin.

"I know these aren't easy questions, but the answers will help me do my job. How often did your mom hit you?"

He looked out the window, not wanting to face me. Feeling ashamed for something that was never his fault.

"She got mad a lot after my dad died."

"Like, once a week?"

"Every couple days I guess. I tried to be good," he whispered, wiping his nose on his sleeve again, in spite of the pile of napkins in his lap.

"It's not your fault," I said. "Your mom and your aunt probably hit you because their parents hit them."

Scott looked up at me, a timid spark of hope in his eyes. "How do you know that?" he asked.

"I've studied a lot about what makes people do things," I said, "and all the books I've read say that if people get hit by their parents, they'll probably hit their own kids."

"Really?"

"That doesn't mean *you* have to," I added. "Everything is a choice." Probably too much for a nine-year old to fathom, but what the hell. Maybe years later he'd look back on this conversation and it would make a difference.

Buddy pawed at Scott's forearm, begging for another bite of whatever was being eaten, and the tension was broken. I had what I needed on the tape. It would be enough to convince Bill that the killings might be related.

At 12:45 I drove Scott back to school. When we were a few blocks away he said, "Did the police tell you anything?"

This was the question I'd been dreading. I'd tried to think of a way not to tell him until it was over, but he was the client and he had certain rights. Plus, he deserved the same level of honesty he'd shown me today. I pulled to the curb.

"Three other people who hurt children were killed recently," I began. "Two of them went to jail for that, but they got out again." I waited for that to sink in. It took a minute.

"You're saying someone killed my mom because she was hurting me?" He looked devastated.

"I'm not sure yet, but maybe. It's not your fault, Scott. You didn't make your mom hit you and you didn't make her yell at you."

I could see the wheels turning as he considered what I was saying. "I hope you're right," he said.

I drove the remaining distance to the school, parking down the street so no one would see him get out of my car.

As he opened the car door he turned back to me. "Thank you," he said. Then he reached back and ruffled Buddy's ears. "See you later, Buddy," he said. "I'll call you tomorrow... Nikki," and he grinned.

I figured if he could still smile I hadn't done too much damage.

CHAPTER 8

N INA'S DATA ENTRY JOB ALLOWED her
unlimited access to registered sex offender
records. She had killed four pedophiles so
far. Defending abused children had become
her mission.

Her first kill had been only two months
ago. His name was Lawrence Novacek. She
had read his file and discovered he was Czech,
like her father, so he seemed a natural choice.
Novacek had just been released from prison.
She knew he'd be hungry.

Nina had purchased a blonde wig and
some oversized sunglasses, and parked outside
Novacek's hotel every morning, following him
when he went out, observing his daily routine.
He would stroll slowly past the local grade
school and then stop outside a daycare center
on Middlefield Road, undoubtedly hoping

one of the kids would wander into range. He didn't have a car, but there was a park across the street where the restrooms were unlocked during the day. It was only a matter of time before he swept some unsuspecting toddler into a vacant stall.

Nina carried a taser, which she planned on using to silence and immobilize Novacek before killing him with the stiletto. She enjoyed the symbolism of killing sexual predators with a knife. Although guns were also phallic, it was the bullets that did the penetrating. That made the act too impersonal. Nina's reason for killing was very personal. The knife blade was coated with garlic to keep the blood from coagulating, and it was long enough to reach the heart of even the most corpulent pedophile. A Sicilian classmate of Nina's had written a short story about the Mafia, which was where she had gotten the garlic idea.

She'd been surprised at how easy it was to kill Novacek. She'd hit him with the taser from behind and he'd dropped to the ground. When he stopped twitching, she'd rolled him over onto his back and forced the stiletto into his heart. A few hours with Gray's Anatomy had taught her a lot. She'd studied the diagrams of the human body in an effort to determine the most efficient way to take a life.

After killing him, she had barely made it home before vomiting convulsively. Then she had slept for ten hours and for the first time in three years there had been no dreams.

Her second kill had been Juan Fernandez, who had served four years at FCI Lompoc for raping his nine-year-old niece. When he got out he had moved into his mother's house in Sunnyvale. He was registered with the police department and had weekly appointments with his parole officer and a court-appointed shrink.

Nina drove to Sunnyvale early one morning and waited for Fernandez to come out of his mother's house, then followed him to a local park. He hovered behind a tree and watched two little girls playing on the swings. When their mother was distracted he'd approached the girls and talked to them briefly, then he went back behind the tree again. Fernandez was wearing a calf-length raincoat. His hands were busy inside the pockets.

The next morning his mother found him dead. Fernandez had made the mistake of sleeping with his window open. Nina had slipped through the open window, put a pillow over his face, and stabbed him in the throat. It had been messy, but exhilarating. She was wearing disposable gloves, a ski mask, and shoe covers. She'd burned her clothes in the backyard when she got home.

Her third kill had been Zogg. She'd been doing research online and found an old newspaper article. After reading the journalist's interview with the molested child's parents, she had accessed the DMV database and located Zogg in San Mateo. The rest was easy.

The fourth was a woman shopping at Mervyn's. That one had been spontaneous and she almost regretted it. Nina had been on her way to housewares when she heard the woman yelling at her young son. Children shouldn't have to grow up hearing such hateful words directed at them, being abused by the people who were supposed to protect them. Still, verbal abuse wasn't sexual. She'd begun carrying the garlic-coated knife with her at all times. Hearing the woman shout at her little boy, Nina had been flooded with rage and, for a few moments, as long as it took to kill, she'd lost control.

CHAPTER 9

I WATCHED BILL'S EXPRESSIONLESS COP'S FACE as he listened to the tape of my conversation with Scott Freedman. I knew what he was feeling only because I know what kind of man he is. When the tape ended he reached for the recorder and hit the rewind button.

"You know this can't be used in court," he said.

"Yeah, I know."

"So what do you expect me to do?" He was angry, but not with me.

"What can anyone do if his aunt is beating him and he has no other family to take him in?" It was a rhetorical question.

The tape finished rewinding and Bill popped it out of the recorder. "Do you mind if I keep this?" he asked.

"Of course not. Will it help?"

"Probably not." He rose from the settee and went into the galley. "You want a Guinness?"

I followed him and wrapped my arms around him from behind as he reached into the refrigerator.

"You're a good person," I murmured.

"Why?" he asked, still angry.

"Because you care."

He turned around and looked at me gravely. "I'll talk to the Captain. See what he thinks. Maybe play the tape for him."

"Will this change the way you look at Scott's mom's murder?"

"Yes. Thank you for that."

I smiled, even though this whole case made my heart ache.

"You're welcome."

Wednesday morning Scott called me collect at 8:15.

"Hi, Nikki." He sounded subdued.

"What's wrong?" I asked, immediately thinking his cousins must have ratted him out to his aunt, who probably used that damn yardstick again. "Are you okay?"

"I guess," he said.

"Did your aunt find out you left school at lunch yesterday?"

"Yeah."

"Did she hit you again?" I can't help it. I'm nosy.

"Um, yeah."

"Do you have any other family you can stay with, Scott?"

"I don't think so."

"I can call Child Welfare. They could put you in a foster home with people who won't hurt you. It would be better than going through this every day."

He was silent for so long that I thought he might have hung up.

"Scott? Are you still there?"

"I'm here. I don't know if I want to do that."

The devil you know is better than the devil you don't.

"Okay," I said. "But will you think about it? I want to help, if you'll let me."

"Did you find out anything new?"

This kid would make a good cop. He was already an expert at compartmentalizing his feelings and changing the subject.

"Not yet," I said. "Sorry. Sometimes it's a slow process. Will you call me tomorrow?"

"Okay. How's Buddy?"

I looked down at Buddy, who was lying at my feet. His chin was on the floor, but his eyes were on me and his brows were raised.

"Buddy's good. You wanna say hi?"

"On the phone?"

"Sure. He won't answer, but I can hold the phone out so he can hear you."

"Okay."

I held the phone near Buddy's face. While Scott was talking, he appeared to listen intently, cocking his head to one side and then the other, occasionally licking the receiver. After a few minutes I wiped the phone on my jeans and raised it to my ear.

"I love you, Buddy," Scott whispered.

I waited a beat then held the phone away from me and said, "Okay, Buddy, that's enough." Into the phone I said, "He licked the receiver a lot. Could you hear?"

"I could hear him breathing. He's a good dog."

"Is your aunt picking you up from school again today?"

"No."

"You want a ride home? Buddy and I could come get you."

I wanted to see where Scott was living, and I wanted to get a look at the aunt.

"That'd be *great!*"

"Okay. What time?"

"I have detention today, so four o'clock?"

"The same place we picked you up before?"

"Yeah."

When we ended the call I looked down at Buddy. "Satisfied?"

He nudged my leg with his nose. I guessed that meant yes. Either that or he was ready for a walk. I hooked his leash to his collar and we went outside.

It was cold, but the sun was shining and the marina landscape was beautiful, even in the winter. Since moving aboard I've learned to appreciate things that grow in the ground. I kind of miss having a garden. Some of my neighbors have planter boxes on their decks, but for me that would negate the freedom of being able to untie my home and sail off to the next place I might want to live.

As we walked around the marina grounds I thought about Scott and what his life must have been like. His dad was dead, his mom used to hit him and now she was dead, and he was living with two cousins who didn't like him and an aunt who resented him enough to hit him with a yardstick. I would have to do something about that. No matter what happened with the case, I wouldn't be able to walk away knowing Scott was being abused.

At lunchtime Buddy and I drove to San Mateo and I did a restaurant survey for one of my regular clients. I brought Buddy a diced chicken breast in a to-go box as a reward for waiting in the car.

After lunch I did some grocery shopping, picking up rice cakes, salad ingredients, and a carrot cake with cream cheese frosting— Bill's favorite. I dropped everything off on the boat, then went to the office and typed up the survey.

At 3:00 Buddy and I took another walk around the marina and then drove to Millbrae. We parked in front of the school at 3:47. I got a paperback out of my gym bag and sat in the front seat reading until Scott came out. I looked up when Buddy started chuffing.

Scott jumped in the front seat and turned around to say hi to Buddy, who washed his face, eliciting a cascade of giggles.

I started the engine. "Buckle up," I said.

Scott gave Buddy one last pet, then turned around to put on his seatbelt. I pulled away from the curb.

"Where to?" I asked.

For some reason I felt nervous waiting for his response. Maybe I was crossing a line. I was conducting an investigation for a nine-year-old orphan, I was chauffeuring him around, he was falling in love with my dog, and I was about to find out where he lived with his abusive aunt.

"Make a left up here," he pointed.

Being a typical male, Scott was not going to give me the directions all at once. He was going to tell me where to go moments before each turn was required. I hate that. I bit my lip and tried to let him direct me in his own way. This took a lot of self-control, but I didn't want to be one more adult giving him a hard time.

We drove two blocks and made another left, then drove five blocks and made a right. By now we were up in the hills, almost to Highway 280. I didn't bother to look at the street names. I'd make a note of the address when we got there.

After the last right turn I had driven about a block when Scott shouted, "Stop!" He sounded alarmed, so I slammed on the breaks and pulled to the curb. He put up his hands trying to hide his face. *"Shit!"*

"What?" I asked.

Scott slid down as far as his seatbelt would allow, but his head was still visible above the dash. He pointed with a trembling index finger and said, "That's my aunt."

I looked up and saw a large, angry-looking woman barreling across the street toward my car. I opened my door to get out, then turned back and said, "Buddy, stay." I closed the car door behind me, but my window was open, a concession to the dog in my life.

The tub of anger approaching me was only a few yards away and pointing a stubby finger at Scott. She was about my height but at least two hundred pounds. Her hair was blond with dark roots, her make-up was excessive, and her jeans were too tight. That probably accounted for the red face.

"What the *fuck* is my *nephew* doing in your *car?*" she yelled.

I took out my cell phone and dialed 911, and then politely said, "I gave him a ride home from school."

She had reached me now and stood so close I could smell her deodorant failing.

"Get out of the car, Scottie, *now!*" she screamed.

I heard the car door open and turned to my young client. "Would you stay in the car for a minute please, Scott? I'd like to have a word with your aunt."

"You can go straight to hell, lady. What are you, some kind of kiddie molester? You like 'em young?" And she shoved me.

I had expected this and I was braced, but she put her weight into it and I stumbled back, banging into the car. I heard Buddy growl deep in his throat and hoped he'd stay put. I did not need a lawsuit involving my dog. As it was, I could have her arrested for assault. If my dog happened to bite her, then I'd be the one in trouble.

The highway patrol 911 operator came on the line and I said, "There's an assault taking place. Scott, what's the address here?"

I was trying to stay calm, but I could feel the adrenaline doing its job. I wanted to fight back.

When she grabbed for my cell phone, I quickly tossed it to Scott. She pushed me out of her way, trying to get at Scott through the open window. Buddy jumped into the front seat and uttered the most ferocious bark I have ever heard in my life. He stopped short of biting her, but he showed his teeth and she quickly backed away from the car.

Scott spoke into the phone, clearly stating the address for the 911 dispatcher.

His aunt turned back to me. "Who the

fuck do you think you *are*?" she shouted,
and gave me another shove.

Buddy leaned out the window, roared
out another bark, and snapped at her. I
quickly stepped between them.

"My name," I said, "is Nicoli Hunter.
I'm a private investigator, and if you touch
me again I'm going to press charges."

She froze. People who abuse children,
for that matter people who routinely break
the law, tend to become alert in the presence
of any kind of cop, even a private cop. She
didn't know what I was investigating. Maybe
she was breaking more laws than I knew
about. Maybe I should make it my business
to find out. I had every intention of pressing
assault charges, but she didn't need to know
that until the cops arrived. In situations
like this I like nothing better than to see an
officer of the law.

I had a small canister of defense spray
on my key chain. I reached into the car and
took my keys out of the ignition, removed
the canister from its case, shook it to activate
it, and pointed the nozzle at the bitch, my
finger poised to spray.

Two boys had come out of a house across
the street and were standing in the front
yard watching. These were the kids I'd seen

following Scott out of the school building. They looked like their mother. Both had dark hair and round bodies. I felt sorry for them, but they were not my concern at the moment.

"Are the police on the way?" I asked Scott.

When he didn't answer I turned my head and quickly glanced into the car. He was still talking. The 911 dispatcher had engaged him in conversation and he was telling her everything that was happening. Excellent! The whole conversation would be recorded and there would be no way his aunt could dispute the assault charges. Now all I had to do was avoid getting my ass kicked and keep my dog in line until the cops arrived.

Scott's aunt recovered the power of speech and, hands on hips, repeated, "What the fuck are you doing with my *nephew?*"

"I don't think that's any of your business," I said, gripping my defense spray and preparing to restrain Buddy if she pushed me again.

Since childhood I have struggled with my inability to back away from confrontations. This is sometimes a problem, like when a woman who outweighs me by sixty-five pounds takes a swing at me.

"I'm *making* it my business," she said, and poked me in the chest.

"This is pepper spray," I said, hoping the 911 dispatcher would catch it. "If you touch me again I'm going to spray it in your face."

She stepped back, but I could tell she wasn't finished. "You have no fucking *right!*" she screamed at me.

No right? "No right to do what?" I asked.

She sputtered and her face looked like it was ready to explode, but she didn't answer. This woman reminded me of a schoolyard bully. She didn't know why she was angry, but the anger was in control.

At long last I heard a siren. It was a beautiful sound. The black and white rolled around the corner and I waved frantically, trying to get their attention. They sped up the street and stopped behind my car and I realized that I didn't know what I was going to say to them. I didn't have Scott's permission to tell anyone that I was working for him, not to mention any of the things he'd told me about his aunt.

I quickly ducked into the car, leaning around Buddy. "Scott, I need your permission to tell the police that your aunt has been hitting you."

I held my breath and waited for him

to respond. Instead he handed me the cell phone and got out of the car. He marched around the back of the car, avoiding his aunt, and approached the police officers, one male and one female, who were now out of the cruiser and talking to Godzilla. She was pointing a finger at me and I heard the word *kidnapper*.

Scott put his hand on the arm of the lady cop to get her attention, and quietly said, "That's a lie."

She turned to look at him and his aunt lunged, cuffing him on the ear before any of us could stop her. Like a flash Buddy flew through the open car window and landed, paws first, on her shoulder. She fell to the ground with the dog on top of her, his teeth bared in her face. I put up my hand to stop the police from approaching, gently pulled him off the woman, and herded him back into the car.

"Good dog," I murmured.

When Buddy was secured, I turned to Scott. "Are you all right?" I asked.

He was rubbing his ear, which was crimson, but he was smiling brightly at Buddy. "I'm okay," he said to me. "Nikki works for me," he said to the cops.

That raised a couple of eyebrows.

The lady cop helped Scott's aunt to her feet and locked her in the back of the patrol car. Then we were able to talk without the threat of another violent outburst. Scott told them about hiring me to investigate his mom's murder. I admired the way they listened, nodding and taking notes as he spoke. Showing him the respect he deserved.

After the police were satisfied that I had a legitimate reason to be chauffeuring Scott around, they asked if I wanted to press charges. I did, and Scott voluntarily told them about the beatings he had suffered since moving in with his aunt.

When we were finished giving our statements, I suggested to the officers that Scott stay with me until other arrangements could be made. This was apparently unacceptable because I wasn't a family member. They said Scott would be placed with San Mateo County Child Protective Services. I didn't feel reassured by this. I wanted to know he was safe and well fed, and that no one was going to hurt him again.

When the CPS unit arrived they collected Scott's cousins, and agreed to let me have a minute alone with Scott before they took him away.

We stood on the passenger side of

my car, petting Buddy through the open window while we talked. I asked if Scott knew his father's first name. He had said his father was dead, but there might be other family members on his father's side. Unfortunately, he couldn't remember. I gave him my smartphone and asked him to hide it in his pocket in case Child Protective Services didn't approve of children having cell phones. I made sure he knew how to turn it on and off, and how to make a call.

"You can call me at the office or at home," I said, pressing one of my cards with my home number printed on the back into his hand.

"Okay," he said. "Thanks, Nikki."

Then he hugged me and I almost lost it. Nine years old, abused by at least two adults, and still willing to trust. He leaned into the car and hugged Buddy before leaving.

When Buddy and I were alone I realized my heart was racing. I longed for a cigarette. I just sat there in the car, petting my dog and breathing deeply. When I felt calm enough to drive, I hightailed it back to the office and called Bill on his cell. I left him a voicemail message telling him everything that had happened. This took a while.

I typed up a detailed report of the

incident, printed two copies, and then called the Millbrae stationhouse. I needed to go in and file an official report in order to press assault charges. If I was lucky, they might tell me what was happening with Scott.

I had noted the female cop's name, and I asked for her when the operator at the PD answered.

"Officer Vasquez is unavailable," she said. "Would you like her voicemail?"

It's a mechanized world.

"Yes, please."

I left Maria Vasquez a message saying I was on my way in to file the report, and that I would appreciate a moment of her time while I was there.

Buddy and I were on our way to the parking lot when he suddenly started spinning in circles on the lawn. After a moment I caught on. He had heard Bill's car in the distance. I turned and spotted the red Mustang approaching on the frontage road. I had to drag Buddy to my car so I could unlock the doors. He wasn't happy about the prospect of getting in the car when Bill was only moments away.

Bill pulled into the parking space next to mine and hopped out. He left the car door open and moved quickly to my side, resisting Buddy's attempt to leap into his arms.

"Are you okay?" he asked, holding me by the shoulders and looking me over.

"I'm fine."

"I got your message," he said.

I'd left the voicemail about twenty minutes earlier, saying I was going to file assault charges against Scott's aunt. He must have jumped to the conclusion that I had been injured.

"I'm okay, but it would be great if you could take Buddy for a while."

Hearing his name, Buddy renewed his efforts. He jumped up and managed to levitate long enough to lick Bill's face before landing back on all fours.

Bill smiled down at him. "I have to go back to work, but I don't think anyone will mind having him in the office."

"Thanks. I don't know how long this might take, and he hates waiting in the car."

"You want me to pick something up for dinner?"

"Sausage and mushroom pizza, with extra cheese."

He pulled me close and kissed me, and I felt my body respond to the kiss. Pizza wouldn't be the only thing on the menu tonight.

CHAPTER 10
◌◌◌

NINA JEZEK HAD CHOSEN HER next target.
She never thought of them as victims.
They were rabid animals that needed to be
put down.

The next to die would be Joshua Crafford.
She had found him in the registry. He'd been
out of jail for two years now and had probably
molested dozens of innocent children in that
time. When Crafford was seventeen he'd been
caught in the act of sodomizing an eight-year
old boy. The child had been riding his bicycle
on Skyline Boulevard and Crafford had pulled
him off the bike and dragged him into the
bushes. Luckily a middle-aged couple had been
walking by and heard the boy crying while
Crafford raped him. The man had beaten the
shit out of Crafford while his wife called the
cops on her cell phone.

Nina knew the kid would never feel good about himself again. He was damaged now, just like she was. It was too late for her to save him, but she could make sure Crafford had no future victims.

Because Joshua Crafford had been seventeen when he was arrested, he was tried as a juvenile. He was sentenced to seven years, instead of three or four, because he had also been convicted of child abduction.

Nina had followed him a couple of times. She knew where he lived and that he worked out at the Powerhouse Gym in Redwood City every morning. Probably wanted to stay fit so he could easily subdue little boys. Nina had purchased a one week visitor's pass. She would be at the gym when he arrived tomorrow. She planned to follow him into the locker room and kill him in the shower. Her hair was short and if she went without make-up and wore a watch cap and oversized sweats, she might pass for a man.

Nina visualized how it would happen and the adrenaline began to flow.

CHAPTER 11

I LOCATED THE MILLBRAE POLICE
DEPARTMENT easily, thanks to directions
from Bill. I have a GPS app on my
smartphone, but I'd given that to Scott.
The PD was housed in a long, low building
surrounded by lawn in the City Hall complex
on Magnolia.

I entered the lobby, approached a reception desk, and asked for Maria Vasquez.
Twenty minutes later she came out to the
lobby. She greeted me stiffly, calling me Ms.
Hunter, shook my hand firmly, and escorted
me back to her desk. We completed a standard assault and battery report.

When we were finished she said, "Scott
told us what you're doing for him."

I raised an eyebrow and said nothing.

"You have kids?" she asked.

"No. Just the dog."

"He told us what happened to his mom. Your investigation means a lot to him."

I wondered where this was going.

"So how much are you charging him?"

There it was. "He gave me some change," I said, perhaps a little brusquely. "Are we finished here?" I stood up and slung my purse strap over my shoulder.

She held up her hand. "Wait a minute," she said. "I didn't mean to offend you. I just hate to see kids taken advantage of. I'm sorry."

Her apology did little to appease me, but at least she had made the effort.

"I feel the same way," I said. "So what happens to Scott now?"

"He's with Children and Family Services. They'll place him in a temporary foster home. After they complete the investigation into the aunt's behavior, he'll probably become available for adoption. Do you know if he has any family besides the aunt?"

"I'm looking into it," I said.

I had planned to do some digging when I had the time. Now I'd have to make it a priority. I felt the same way about Scott being in a foster home as I'd felt about

Buddy being in a cage at the Humane Society before I adopted him. Not good.

It was after 6:00 by the time I got back to the marina. I unlocked the office and called Bill on his cell while I booted up the computer.

"Anderson."

"Hunter."

"Hey, babe. Are you back from Millbrae?"

"I am. Where are you?"

"I'm still at the office. It's hard to get anything done with everyone gathered around petting Buddy."

"What do you think? Is he police dog material?"

"Not a chance."

"I need some information from you. Okay to talk on the cell?"

"I'll come to your office. I'm just about done here anyway."

When we hung up I listened to my voicemail. There were no messages from Scott. I called my home number and keyed in the voicemail code. No messages there either. He probably hadn't been alone long enough to call, or he'd called and hadn't left a message.

Bill and Buddy arrived fifteen minutes later. As they came into the office Buddy

81

tugged the leash out of Bill's hand and galloped over to me. He climbed halfway onto my lap and licked my face enthusiastically. I wiped off the slobber and smiled up at Bill. He was holding a binder.

"What's that?" I asked.

"I thought you might want more information about the Freedman killing."

He was apparently loosening up when it came to sharing confidential information.

"You were right. I need to do a search for family members. Scott's going into temporary foster care, and I want to make sure he doesn't go back to his aunt. Do you have his mom's social security number?"

Bill opened the binder and read it to me. I typed an e-mail request to Criminal Investigative Services, the company I use for background checks, asking for a family tree on Gloria and any spouse they could find a record of. I was hoping Scott's deceased dad might have family nearby, maybe a brother or a sister who would be suitable.

I sent the e-mail and turned back to Bill. Silently, he handed over the binder, watching as I read the contents. There was nothing significant that he hadn't already told me.

"Where's my pizza?" I asked, passing the binder back to him.

"I called *Pizza and Pipes* from the car. Should be here in half an hour."

"Just enough time."

Everything tastes better after sex. We ate pizza at the galley counter and I tossed bits of sausage to Buddy. I told Bill the whole story about what had happened with Scott's aunt, and how Buddy had defended me vocally and Scott physically, without actually biting anyone. He patted the dog's head and rewarded him with a small bite of carrot cake.

◠ ◡ ◠

On Thursday morning I got up early and went to the gym. After working out I hurried back to the boat to retrieve Buddy before Bill left for work.

I was in the office by 7:45. I opened my e-mail first thing, and was surprised to find the report from CIS on Scott's family tree. I read the soft copy as the report was printing.

Scott's father, Don Freedman, had died in a car accident six years ago. Don's father had passed away two years ago, and his mother just last year. I wondered if Scott had spent any time with his paternal grandparents before they'd passed. Don's father had only one sibling, a sister named Roselyn, who was also deceased, but she had been married to a man named Jack Verne Trusty, now sixty-two, who lived in Seattle. Jack and Roselyn had no children. I wondered if that was by choice.

I Googled Jack V. Trusty in Seattle, and clicked on the white pages link, took a deep breath, and dialed.

"Trusty and Associates," said a sultry female voice.

"This is Nicoli Hunter calling for Jack Trusty."

"I'm sorry, Ms. Hunter. Mister Trusty is in the field today. Would you like his voicemail?"

"I would, but first can you tell me what kind of firm Trusty and Associates is?"

There was a momentary hesitation before she said, "We're a private investigation firm. We specialize in criminal background checks, security surveys, and executive protection. If you didn't know that, why are you calling?"

Scott's great uncle was a PI? What are the odds?

"I'm not calling to hire Jack," I said.

"I'm calling because his great nephew, Scott, has been orphaned."

"Oh, I'm so sorry. I'll transfer you to his voicemail."

I left Jack a brief message saying I wanted to talk to him about Scott, and left my office and home phone numbers. They had probably never met, but there was no time like the present. Seattle wasn't that far away. He could hop on a commuter flight and be here in a couple of hours.

I looked through the remaining pages of the report and found that Gloria Freedman's maiden name had been Kimball. Her sister's name was Leah Mohr, and she was divorced. Gloria's parents, Michael and Anna Kimball, were living in Florida. I thought about the fact that both of their daughters had a penchant for child beating. I'd wait to hear back from Jack before I even considered approaching them.

I Googled Trusty and Associates and located the website. There was a picture of Jack on the home page. His face was round and he had a bushy mustache that covered his upper lip. He was built like a fireplug and looked every one of his sixty-two years, but there was a twinkle in his eyes and he had a kind smile. In the photo he was wearing a trench coat and a fedora cocked at an angle reminiscent of Humphrey Bogart in *The Maltese Falcon*. He had a sense of humor. Also in the photo was a bull terrier seated at his feet. A sense of humor, and he liked dogs. Excellent!

I spent the rest of the morning and early afternoon doing restaurant surveys and feeding Buddy my leftovers. When we got back to the office I had a voicemail message from Scott.

"Hi, Nikki. I'm okay. I'll call you later. Say hi to Buddy for me."

I thought about calling him back, but if he was in school or in a social services office somewhere, I didn't want him to get in trouble for carrying the cell phone.

I typed up the surveys I'd done and sent them off, then decided to take a look at the Department of Justice website that Bill had told me about. It was apparent that someone out there intended to eliminate as many child abusers as possible. If I could locate the worst registered sex offenders in the Bay Area, maybe I could stake them out and catch the killer in the act. Of course, I had no idea how many serious offenders there might be on the Peninsula, but I didn't think there could be that many.

I searched online for the DOJ and found a web page entitled Megan's Law – Information on Registered Sex Offenders. After agreeing to the stipulations for accessing the information I was allowed to do a search for registered sex offenders. I entered Redwood City and selected the registrants page. There were six pages containing one hundred and fifteen sex offenders, their photographs, their addresses, and lists of the crimes they had committed. I was stunned by the number, and by how available the information was. Of the one hundred and fifteen, four were women. That didn't really surprise me, but it made me think.

I started reading, printing out any file listing habitual sexual abuse of children. According to Bill, the predators shown on this website were the serious and high-risk sex offenders. The lower level offenders' records were not accessible to the public. The age range of these criminals was wide, and all ethnic groups were represented, but as I looked at each photograph I noticed that many of them had something in common. There was no conscience behind their eyes. Some even looked proud or were smiling in their mug shots. These were people who didn't believe cultural boundaries and laws applied to them, with no regard for the consequences of their actions and a complete lack of empathy for the suffering of the children they victimized. There might be pedophiles out there who felt remorse for the disturbing things they were compelled to do, but I saw no evidence of that in these website photos.

It took me almost two hours to read all the files and by the time I was finished I had a headache and felt like I needed a shower. Twenty of the registrants in Redwood City were child molesters and five of those had habitual sexual abuse of children in their files. All five were men. Jonathan Franklin Lewis, Gabriel Adamson, Timothy Vasey, Nicholas Edward Tooker, and Pablo Fabian Morales.

I spread the printed registry pages across my desk and was looking at the five faces when my phone rang. I picked up the receiver, distracted by all that I had read that afternoon.

"Hunter Investigations."

"Hi, Nikki." It was Scott.

"Hi, Scott. How are you? *Where* are you?"

"I'm at a foster home in Burlingame. There's six kids here."

"How are they treating you?"

"Okay, I guess."

"Will you be going back to school tomorrow?"

"Yeah, but they haven't decided where yet. I was going to Hoover in Redwood City until I moved in with my aunt. She said I had to go to Spring Valley, 'cause she wasn't driving me to Redwood City every day. The kids who live here go to Franklin, so I think maybe I'll go there too."

"That's good," I said. "Then you won't have to see your cousins."

"I know. How's Buddy?"

"Buddy's good. Call me from school tomorrow and we'll come see you on your lunch break."

"That'd be cool. Any news about my mom?"

"I've been doing some background research. I'm also looking for other family members you could live with. Tell me about your mom's parents. Did you ever spend any time with them?"

"Nope. Mom said she wouldn't wish her parents on a dog. I guess that means she didn't like 'em very much."

"What about your Uncle Jack?"

"Who?"

"Your dad's father had a sister who was

married to a guy named Jack Trusty. Did you ever meet him?"

"I never even heard of him. I don't remember my dad. He died when I was little."

"Okay. Call me tomorrow?"

"I will. Hey, can you bring the charger for this phone? The battery is low."

Smart kid. I hadn't even thought of that. "I'll stick it in my purse right now. See you tomorrow, Scott, and thanks for calling."

"Say hi to Buddy for me?"

I promised that I would.

After we hung up I unplugged the cell phone charger and dropped it into my purse. When I got a chance, I'd have to visit Radio Shack and pick up a prepaid cell to trade Scott for my smartphone.

CHAPTER 12

AT 6:00 P.M. BUDDY AND I closed the office and went for another walk. We eventually strolled down to the dock, and as we reached the bottom of the companionway I looked over at Elizabeth's trawler—lights out, door closed. Since becoming engaged to Jack McGuire, retired cat burglar and former client of mine, she was spending more evenings at his estate in Hillsborough. I was happy for them, but I missed having her at the marina all the time. Maybe I'd give her a call and see if we could get together again this weekend.

Buddy and I stopped to visit with D'Artagnon who was outside on the deck of his owner's Bluewater 42. When I adopted Buddy I'd worried that there might be

Nancy Skopin

some jealousy issues, but the two dogs had bonded instantly.

We continued down the dock and boarded my boat. I grabbed a Guinness from the galley fridge before wandering into the main salon, which is like my living room. It's also where I keep my telephone. The voicemail light was blinking, so I pressed play.

The message was from Jack Trusty. It was brief and to the point.

"This is J.V. Trusty. I got your message about Scott. I've never met the boy, but you can call me back anytime." He left his cell number.

I liked the sound of his voice and the fact that he was willing to give his cell number to a total stranger. Of course he was a PI. He'd probably checked me out before returning my call. I picked up the phone and dialed. Jack answered on the second ring.

"Trusty and Associates."

"This is Nicoli Hunter."

"Oh yes, Scott's friend. How is he?"

"Well, as I mentioned in my voicemail he's an orphan now. His mother was murdered two weeks ago."

"How do you know Scott, Miss Hunter?"

"Please, call me Nikki."

"Okay, Nikki. How do you know Scott?"

"He hired me to find out who killed his mom."

"I understand you're a licensed PI."

"That's right."

"Small world."

"I know. After his mom was killed, Scott was taken in by his aunt, Gloria's sister. But Gloria's sister was beating him with a yardstick. In fact, she assaulted me when I drove him home from school. She's in custody at the moment and Scott's in foster care. I did some research and found out that you and Gloria's parents are Scott's only other family. According to Scott, Gloria wouldn't let her parents near him. I think they were abusive when she was a kid. Anyway, I hate to see him go into the system. There's no telling what kind of people he'd end up with. He's a great kid and he's already been through so much." I took a breath. "So I was thinking maybe you could fly down and meet him. See if you hit it off."

"Jesus *Christ.* I'm sixty-*two.*"

"I know how old you are. What's your point?"

"Well Scott must be, what, eight or nine now?"

"He's nine."

"By the time he's twenty I'll be seventy-three."

"He doesn't need someone young to look after him, Mr. Trusty. He needs someone kind. Someone who won't slap him around. Just meet him. That's all I'm asking. Please?"

"Call me J.V. You're pretty stubborn, aren't you?"

"Does that mean you'll come?"

"I'll call you back with my flight information."

"Great! Thank you."

"I'm not making any promises."

When we hung up I grabbed Buddy and gave him a hug. I had to hug someone and Bill was at work. With any luck J.V. would be here by the weekend, and if they liked each other he could file the adoption papers next week.

Bill called a little after seven and I couldn't wait to tell him the news, so I invited him over. I showed him Scott's family tree and we booted up his laptop so I could show him J.V.'s website. He was less enthusiastic than I'd hoped he would be.

"You're treading on dangerous ground here, Nikki," he said, always the cop. "When you get involved in other people's lives you risk making a mess of them."

"You get involved in other people's lives every day. Besides, all I plan to do is introduce them. J.V. seems like a nice guy, and things can't get any worse for Scott."

"Sure they can. What if they get along great and Scott grows to depend on him, and then he gets sick or something?"

"You always look at the dark side," I snapped. "J.V.'s only sixty-two. He appears to be in good health." I pointed to his photo on the web page. "He's family, and he has a dog. I think this could work."

Buddy got up from his spot on the floor and lifted my elbow with his nose. His eyes were bright and his tail was wagging slowly. I could tell he was distressed by my tone of voice. I decided there was no point in arguing with Bill about this. I was just upset because he didn't see things my way.

"I'll make dinner," I said.

I scooped kibble into Buddy's dish, freshened up his water, and made a couple of steak salads for myself and Bill. We didn't talk about Scott again that night, but I took the argument to bed with me and didn't sleep well.

Friday morning I woke to the sound

of rain hammering on the deck. I dragged myself out of bed, made a pot of Kona coffee, and took a thermal mug with me to the gym. I did my usual upper body workout and then jogged on the treadmill for thirty minutes.

When I got back to the boat at 7:30, Bill was holstering his Glock.

"You're leaving early," I said.

"I have a meeting."

His expression was cloudy and I could guess what he was thinking. Bill and I rarely leave a disagreement unresolved. I just didn't know how to fix this one. I felt in my gut that I was doing the right thing, and he wanted me to be cautious.

"How about this," I said. "I'll meet J.V. first, get to know him a little, and then if I still think it's a good idea I'll introduce him to Scott."

"You *are* a pretty good judge of character."

I smiled. It was as close to a concession as I was going to get.

"Thanks," I said, and wrapped my arms around him.

Buddy and I unlocked the office at 8:00. I went over my schedule of bar and restaurant surveys. I needed to dine at Chez Jacques and Barron's this weekend, and there were four bars that needed my attention between

Burlingame and Mountain View. I decided to take Bill to Chez Jacques tomorrow night if he wasn't working, and then we could survey a couple of the bars together. I could cover everything else on Sunday.

My phone rang at 9:15.

"Hunter Investigations."

"Good morning, Nikki."

"J.V.?"

"Good ear. I'm flying into SFO tomorrow at nine fifty-three a.m." He told me the airline and flight number.

"I'll meet you at baggage claim," I said. "How long will you be here?"

"My return flight is on Sunday afternoon. Can you recommend a hotel?"

"I might be able to do better than that. Let me get back to you."

Bill had been spending a lot of his weekends with me recently, and his two-bedroom house on Madison Avenue was just sitting there, empty. Since J.V. was doing me a favor by flying in to meet with Scott, I thought it would be nice if I could save him the cost of a hotel. I called Bill's office number.

"Anderson."

"Hey. Is your meeting over already?"

"A couple of people didn't show, so we finished early. What's up?"

"I just talked to J.V. Trusty. He's flying in tomorrow morning and he'll be here through Sunday afternoon. He asked if I could recommend a hotel and I was wondering if maybe he could stay at your house tomorrow night."

"Have you run a background check on him yet?"

"I don't have a driver's license or social security number."

"Call you back," he said, and hung up.

Five minutes later my phone rang again. I snatched it up and, before I could offer my usual greeting, Bill read me an eight-digit number, then said, "Call me after you check him out."

Wow! Bill was *really* loosening up about department policy. I normally use CIS for background checks because they're so thorough, but they take at least twenty-four hours to complete a background report including criminal and financial data. In the past I've gotten a faster response by offering more than the usual fee, and by begging. I checked my desktop address book and located their number.

"CIS, this is Leann."

"Leann, it's Nicoli Hunter."

"Hey! How's everything in California?"

"Cold and wet. I need a huge favor. I'll pay extra."

I gave Leann J.V.'s driver's license number and told her what I needed. She said she'd do her best. Leann's best is pretty amazing.

While I was waiting I tidied up the office. I needed to burn some nervous energy. I dusted, wiped out the refrigerator, ran the vacuum, cleaned the kitchen and bathroom sinks, and ran a brush around the toilet bowl.

Scott called me at 10:35 and said he'd be out in front of Franklin Elementary at 12:30. I told him Buddy and I would pick him up and we'd go to McDonald's. He liked that idea, although I imagined he'd be willing to eat almost anything for lunch as long as Buddy came along for the ride.

At 11:20 I checked my e-mail for the hundredth time and found a new message from CIS. I hastily opened the attachment and scanned the document. As always, the date sequence was reversed with the most current activity at the beginning.

J.V. Trusty had owned his own PI firm since 1991. He'd been a licensed PI since 1987. He had made his living as a restaurant and bar owner and as a musician from 1976 through 1986. He was also a volunteer firefighter during those years. He'd been in the Marines from 1971 through 1975, and had received the Medal of Honor for 'conspicuous gallantry and intrepidity in action at the risk of his life above and beyond the call of duty'. He was a decorated war hero! I printed the pages and speed-dialed Bill's cell. I read him the highlights.

"Yeah, okay, he can stay in my house. But the fact that he's a hero doesn't make him a nice guy."

"Thank you."

I called J.V. and got his voicemail.

"J.V., it's Nikki Hunter. My friend has a house here in Redwood City that he isn't using on the weekends, so you're welcome to stay there while you're in town. I'll see you tomorrow morning."

I hung up the phone and wondered if it was too soon to tell Scott his uncle was coming. I didn't want him to be taken by surprise, but I also didn't want him to get his hopes up, in case things didn't work out.

I looked at Buddy. "He has a dog," I said. At the word *dog* Buddy's head came up from the floor, his eyes shining with recognition. "Anyone who loves dogs is okay, right?" He tilted his head to the side. Clearly he agreed with me.

Buddy and I locked up the office and ran through the rain to the parking lot. We drove to the local Radio Shack and I bought a prepaid cell before we went to Burlingame.

We arrived early and sat in the school parking lot waiting for Scott to come out. At 12:28 I popped open my umbrella and got out of the car, standing where he would be able to see me from either door. At 12:31 he came out the side exit and hurried down the steps. Buddy had his head out the car window and he whined softly when he scented Scott. My dog was getting attached to this kid. Hell, *I* was getting attached to him.

We got into the car and I dug the new prepaid cell phone and charger out of my purse while Scott reached back to pet Buddy and then fastened his seatbelt.

"Here's your new phone and charger, and this is your new cell phone number." I handed him a slip of paper on which I'd written the number of the prepaid phone.

He tucked everything into his backpack and handed me my smartphone, then turned in his seat so he could pet Buddy some more on the way to McDonald's. We ordered two Quarter Pounders with cheese, fries, milkshakes, and an apple pie.

"So how's the new school?" I asked.

"It's okay."

"What about the foster home?"

"Everybody's nice, but it's weird. Some of the kids don't talk. It's like they're afraid to say anything. But they have two cats."

"Cats are good."

"Yeah."

"Listen, Scott, I talked to your great uncle today. His name is J.V. Trusty and he lives in Seattle. Do you know where that is?"

"Washington, right?"

"Right. He's a PI, like me."

"Really?"

"Yeah. So, I asked him if he'd fly down here to meet you. I hope that's okay."

"Why?"

"Because you can't go back with your aunt and I didn't think you'd want to stay in a foster home. If you and your uncle like each other maybe you could live with him."

"In Washington?"

"It's not that far away. He has a dog. A bull terrier. And he's a war hero. He was awarded the Medal of Honor."

"That's pretty cool." He'd stopped eating.

"What's wrong?" I asked.

"I don't know. I was thinking maybe I could live with you and Buddy."

He spoke in a whisper, but his words hit me like a fist.

"I think you're great, Scott. But I'd make a terrible parent. It's all I can do to take care of myself and Buddy. Besides, I live on a boat. There isn't a lot of room."

"I wouldn't take up much space."

He looked so forlorn that I almost cried, but I pushed my feelings aside and said, "Your uncle's flying down from Seattle tomorrow morning. I thought the three of us could take Buddy to the park and get to know each other."

"Okay."

"If you give me the phone number of your foster parents, I'll call them to make sure it's all right with them."

He pulled a black nylon wallet out of his pants pocket and took out a slip of paper. He read me the names of his foster parents along with their address and phone number, and I copied everything down.

We both fed Buddy French fries and bites of burger, and when our time was up I drove him back to school. He hugged Buddy and silently climbed out of the car, leaving me with an empty feeling in the pit of my stomach, in spite of the Quarter Pounder.

CHAPTER 13

ON SATURDAY MORNING I LEFT Buddy onboard with Bill and drove to the airport. I parked in the arrivals lot and hiked to the United terminal to check the monitors. J.V.'s flight was on schedule, due to arrive at 9:53. It was only 9:10, so I found a gift shop and browsed through the books. I purchased the latest Lois Greiman mystery, found a vacant seat opposite the United counter, and started reading, periodically checking the monitor to make sure the flight was still on time.

At 9:50 I tucked the book in my purse and walked down to baggage claim. I didn't know if J.V. had checked any luggage, but it had seemed like a convenient place to meet. While I was standing there I remembered I hadn't told him what I looked like. Then

I remembered he was a PI. He'd probably found the newspaper articles with my photo from four months ago, when I'd been charged with murder.

I watched the escalator and recognized J.V. Trusty as soon as he came into view. He was wearing the trench coat I'd seen on his website, without the fedora. His eyes were magnified by a pair of aviator-style glasses, and he was five-seven at the most, with a halo of gray hair. He scanned the area and when his gaze locked onto mine he smiled and his blue eyes lit up.

I stepped forward and offered my hand. His grip was firm, his stare appraising. I liked him instantly.

"You have any luggage?" I asked.

"Just this," he said, hoisting a carry-on bag.

"Why don't we get you settled at the house before we go to meet Scott?"

As we walked to the lot where I was parked I asked how his flight had been.

"It was fine," he said. "I'm not crazy about flying, so I always go first class."

"Must be nice."

We stowed J.V.'s bag in the trunk of the 2002 and motored around to the exit, where I paid for my parking.

During the drive to Redwood City, J.V. asked about two of my recent cases. In July I'd almost been killed by a multiple murderer I was trying to track down, and in August I'd taken the life of a serial killer, in self-defense. J.V. wanted details.

I told him abbreviated versions of both stories and when I finished he said, "You ever decide to move up north, give me a call. I could use somebody like you."

I was flattered, but I didn't want to work for someone else.

"So, the Medal of Honor," I said. "Impressive."

"I don't like to talk about that time in my life," he said. "The war really messed me up. When I got home I wasn't right for a long time."

I let that sit between us for a few minutes before saying, "So you like dogs?"

J.V. looked at me. "You checked out my website?" I nodded. "Her name is Merla. Two years old. She's my fourth bull terrier."

"Scott loves dogs," I offered. "I spoke with his foster parents last night and they're expecting us at noon. I thought we could pick up some fast food and go to the park. I'd like to bring my dog Buddy along, if that's okay with you. He and Scott are crazy about each other."

"Fine with me," he said.

We arrived at Bill's house and I unlocked the door, then handed J.V. the key.

"Aren't you coming in?" he asked.

"Sure."

I gave J.V. a tour of the house and escorted him to the back bedroom where he'd be sleeping. I'd changed the sheets the night before, and stocked the fridge with bottled water, eggs, bacon, vegetables, and a couple of organic chicken breasts.

"I didn't know what you liked to eat or drink," I said, opening the refrigerator.

"I'm not picky," he said.

"I have some restaurant and bar surveys to do tonight," I went on. "I'd love some company, if you feel like coming along."

"Sounds good."

J.V. was watching me as I spoke and I realized that he was doing exactly what I do when I'm analyzing a subject. He was studying me, observing my body language, posture, eye contact, and tone of voice.

"You ever study psychology?" I asked.

"My whole life has been a study of psychology, but no, I never took a class."

I *really* liked this guy.

"So, tell me about my nephew's case," he said.

I thought for a moment about the confidentiality issue. I didn't have Scott's permission to discuss the investigation, but J.V. had a right to know what kind of emotional baggage the kid was carrying.

"I'm pretty sure Gloria, Scott's mom, was killed by someone targeting child molesters," I began. "I don't think Scott was ever molested, but his mom used to spank him a lot and there was a scene at the Mervyn's store where she was killed, right before it happened. She was in the fitting room with Scott, yelling at him. From what I hear, she was pretty harsh. She went to get him another pair of jeans and never came back. By the time he went looking for her, she was already dead. What connects her death to three other local homicides is the weapon. It was a long narrow knife, coated with garlic. Two of the other victims were registered sex offenders. The third never went to trial, but he was accused and charged."

"Garlic huh? So the blood can't clot. That's an old Sicilian trick. You think this killer overheard Scott's mom yelling at him and decided to add her to his list?"

"Or her list, yeah."

"So what are you doing?"

"I spent a couple of hours reading registered sex offender files online. I started with Redwood City because Gloria was killed here and so was the first victim that we know about. There are a hundred and fifteen individuals registered. I narrowed the list by concentrating on those convicted of habitual sexual abuse of children. I have photos and home addresses. I thought I'd stake them out."

"Because they're potential targets for the killer," he said. "How many are there?"

"Five."

"You'll need help."

"Are you volunteering?"

"Maybe."

J.V. and I drove to the marina and I walked him down to the boat. Buddy was sitting in the pilothouse, having heard my car enter the lot, and he started growling when he saw that I was with a stranger. J.V. slowly held out his right hand, palm down, and Buddy crept forward sniffing the air. He wagged his tail and covered the remaining distance between them, then poked his nose into J.V.'s coat pocket. J.V. laughed and pulled out a small dog biscuit.

We descended the companionway into

the galley and I introduced J.V. to Bill. They shook hands, sizing each other up.

I hooked Buddy's leash to his collar, told Bill I'd be back around 3:30, and kissed him on the cheek.

During the drive to Burlingame Buddy spent a lot of time licking the back of J.V.'s ears. J.V. would occasionally reach back and scratch his neck or rub the top of his head, but he never once complained about all the slobber. I hoped he was as good with kids as he was with dogs.

We arrived at the address Scott had given me and found a two-story white clapboard with a small front yard filled with bicycles. There was a Toyota SUV in the driveway and toys cluttered the front porch.

We left Buddy in the car and approached the house. Before we could knock, Scott threw open the door and looked up at J.V. I watched the two of them checking each other out. It reminded me of the way Scott had stood in my office doorway on Monday, looking me over before saying a word.

"Scott, this is your uncle, J.V. Trusty," I said.

J.V. reached out to shake hands. "How ya doin', Scott?"

Scott took his hand, looking very mature for his nine years, and said, "I'm fine, sir."

I said, "Buddy's in the car. You wanna pick up some burgers and go to the park?"

Scott looked at me and then turned to the car. It was drizzling, but I'd left the rear vent window open and Buddy was straining to squeeze his head through.

"I need to tell the Brewsters I'm leaving," he said. "I'll be right back."

Scott was gone only a moment before a blonde woman in her thirties appeared in the doorway, drying her hands on a dishtowel. "You must be Nikki," she said. "Scottie's very fond of you. I'm Ilene Brewster." She held out a damp hand and I shook it. Gentle grip, slightly calloused palm.

"He's a great kid," I said. "This is his Uncle J.V. We're planning to go to McDonald's and then spend some time at Bayside Park. We'll probably be back around three."

"That's fine," she said.

Scott came outside, slipping into a jacket. As he passed Ilene she tousled his hair. She watched us from the doorway as we all piled into the car. Scott climbed in the backseat with Buddy and was smothered with canine kisses as he tried to fasten his seatbelt. As I pulled away from the curb Ilene closed the front door.

"Nice lady," I said to Scott.

"She's okay."

Scott spent the drive to McDonald's getting reacquainted with Buddy.

We all ordered Quarter Pounders with cheese and I got a large order of fries for everyone to share. J.V. ordered lemonade, I ordered iced tea, and Scott opted for a chocolate shake. I passed the bags over to J.V., and Buddy leaned between the seats trying to get closer to the food.

By the time we arrived at the park it had stopped raining. We found a vacant picnic table and I threw the beach towel I keep in my trunk across the bench seat to soak up the water. We ate in silence while Scott and J.V. eyed each other furtively. Buddy made out like a bandit with bites of burger and fries.

After lunch I handed Scott the leash. "You want to walk Buddy around?"

"Sure," he said, beaming as he slipped his small hand through the loop.

I followed a short distance behind Scott, J.V., and Buddy, hoping to give them the illusion of privacy. But I stayed close enough to catch most of their conversation.

J.V. said, "I was sorry to hear about your mom," followed by, "I lost my mamma when I was nine and a half. They let me in to see her at the hospital the night she passed. I guess they knew she was going soon, because kids weren't allowed to visit patients in the hospital back then."

"That's too bad," Scott commented. "Nikki says you're a PI."

J.V. nodded. "Yep."

"You like it?"

"I do. You get to poke around in other people's business and you get to help people. I like helping people."

"You have a dog?"

"I have a bull terrier named Merla. She's two."

"What's a bull terrier look like?"

"Well, she's white with black spots and a long pointy nose, and her head's as hard as a bowling ball."

He pulled a photo out of his wallet and showed it to Scott, who smiled appreciatively before handing it back.

"You play any musical instruments?" J.V. asked.

"I wanted to learn the guitar, but my mom said it was too expensive. Do you?"

"Before I became a PI I used to be in a

band. I play stand-up bass, trombone, and drums. Me and a couple friends get together and jam once in a while."

After a few minutes of this kind of back and forth Buddy stopped to lift his leg on a shrub and Scott looked up at J.V. "What's Seattle like?"

I felt my gut clench. I knew what was coming.

"It's nice. It rains a lot, but the air is fresh and everything is green. Good people."

"You think I'd like it there?"

"I don't see why not."

"Are you going to adopt me?"

There it was. No beating around the bush with this kid. His heart had to be pounding as he waited for his uncle to respond.

"I'll tell you something, Scott. I've learned over the years that other people are the most important thing in my life. So if you think you could stand to live with an old geezer like me, then I think we should give it a try."

Scott looked into J.V.'s face for a long moment, then nodded once and said, "Okay," and we started walking again.

I felt the tension in my solar plexus move up into my heart and clog my throat.

After we'd dropped Scott off at the

Brewster's and were on our way back to Redwood City J.V. said, "I guess I'll extend my stay another day. Get the paperwork started. You know anything about this kind of adoption?"

"Not a clue, but I'm sure social services will be happy to walk you through the process. You're a good man, J.V."

He nodded, looking uncomfortable, and said, "I'm just doing what anyone would do under the circumstances."

I wasn't so sure about that, but I kept my opinion to myself.

CHAPTER 14

JOSHUA CRAFFORD FINISHED HIS LAST set of bench presses and toweled the sweat from his face as he walked to the locker room. Working out always made him horny. He was planning a trip to the zoo that afternoon, hoping to find an unguarded boy to play with. He fantasized about it as he lathered his genitals in the shower. He was slowly stroking his soapy cock when the shower curtain was pulled aside.

"Hey, man! It's occupied!"

Nina stepped into the shower stall and drew the curtain closed behind her.

Crafford said, "Look, buddy, I'm flattered, but you're not my type." Then he took a closer look and said, "What the fuck?"

Nina grabbed him by the windpipe, cutting off his air and immobilizing him. She flicked open the switchblade and jammed it upward through his solar plexus into his heart, all the while staring into his startled brown eyes. It was over so quickly that Crafford was dead before he thought to resist.

Nina rinsed her hands and the knife in the shower before retracting the blade and slipping it back into her pocket. She checked her clothes for blood, but what little there was didn't show on the black sweats she was wearing. She checked to see if she was alone, then exited the stall, quickly pulling the curtain closed behind her. On her way out of the locker room she grabbed a gym towel and pulled it over her head and shoulders to further disguise herself.

Her pulse sped up as she hit the street, walking slowly and occasionally glancing over her shoulder. No one was following. She'd gotten away clean once again.

CHAPTER 15

J.V. AND I DROVE FROM Burlingame, where we'd left Scott, back to my office at the marina. I immediately went online and found the San Mateo County Children and Family Services website. I selected the adoption link and made a note of the phone number, then passed J.V. the number and the phone.

"You want some privacy?"

"Nah. I might need moral support."

I didn't expect anyone at the county offices to be working on the weekend, but I listened as J.V. persuaded the operator who had answered his call to transfer him to Scott's caseworker. He answered questions and asked them, taking notes for maybe fifteen minutes, then he put his hand over the mouthpiece and said, "What's your fax number?"

I told him the number and he repeated it into the phone, said thank you, and hung up.

"They're faxing me the forms," he said, smiling broadly. "They've already made a determination about Scott's aunt, and since I'm a relative they're going hustle me through the adoption process."

"You're excited about this, aren't you?"

"I guess I am. I'm also scared to death, but you were right. He's a great kid."

"You'll be lucky to have each other, J.V."

It would have been an awkward moment if the fax hadn't started ringing.

I called Bill to let him know I'd be tied up a while longer.

J.V. and I spent an hour filling out forms. When we were finished I made copies of everything and we drove to the County Center where Scott's caseworker had agreed to meet us. By the time we left we were both exhausted. I let Buddy out of the car for a quick walk around and offered him some bottled water before we hit the road again.

I dropped J.V. at Bill's house and reminded him we were doing a dinner and two bar surveys that night. "You still up for it?" I asked.

"Sure. Just call me before you come to pick me up. I think I might take a nap."

I didn't blame him. I could use one myself.

Buddy and I motored back to the marina. I felt guilty for leaving him alone in the car for so long, so we walked around the grounds watering shrubbery before going down to the boat.

When we climbed aboard I heard the TV and knew Bill was there. Buddy launched himself down the companionway and scrambled over the hardwood floor into the main salon. I tossed my purse on the galley counter, filled Buddy's kibble dish, and got myself a Guinness before following. Quarter Pounders and beer—I definitely needed more time at the gym.

Buddy had climbed into Bill's lap, ignoring the offered kibble, and Bill was stroking his ears, submitting to puppy kisses, and laughing. The sight of the two males in my life so clearly attached to each other touched my heart. I could never spend time with a man who doesn't love animals as much as I do.

Two months ago, when Bill suggested we cohabitate, his relationship control issues had hit the surface. Even though I'd declined his offer, he'd apparently felt we were "committed," and his demeanor toward me had shifted. I'd never met Bill's parents, but if I had to guess, I'd say his father was dominant in their marriage. Bill had never been married, or even engaged as far as I knew, so he hadn't recognized the pattern. We'd had a minor blow-up about it, but things had finally returned to normal. We would need to have a serious conversation at some point in the future, but for now, as long as I kept him at arm's length, we were good. That wasn't usually a problem for me, but watching him with Buddy made me wonder where we were headed.

"How'd it go with J.V. and Scott?" he asked.

"Great. J.V. filed the adoption papers today."

"On a Saturday? That was fast."

I swallowed some Guinness. "When it's right, it's right."

Bill looked at me. "Are you working tonight?"

"I have three surveys to do. J.V.'s coming with me. You wanna come too?"

"Someone should stay here with the dog."

I finished my Guinness and said, "I need a nap." I gave Bill a lingering kiss filled with promises about what would come later, and headed for the stateroom. I set the Dream Machine alarm for 6:45.

When the alarm went off I rolled out of bed and loaded the coffee maker. I showered and dressed before calling J.V.

"Trusty and Associates," he answered.

"You ready to go?"

"Come and get me."

That night we dined on authentic Spanish cuisine and observed waiters, waitresses, and bartenders. I caught one "no sale," which meant the bartender hadn't recorded the drink order on the register and would pocket the cash. J.V. spotted a busboy wiping his nose with his hand before refilling a customer's water glass. *Gross.*

Over dinner we talked about J.V.'s life experiences, and about mine. He expressed genuine sympathy when I told him about my dad's disappearance and that my mom was a former nun. We talked about the pros and cons of the PI business and, once again, he offered me a position with his firm if I ever decided to move north.

At the end of the evening I had a good feeling about Scott's future. J.V. was a kind-hearted, intelligent realist, and I felt confident he could undo a lot of the damage that had been done to Scott in the last nine years.

When I dropped him off at Bill's house I leaned in for a hug and he gave me a tight squeeze. I didn't plan to work on Sunday, so I said I'd call him in the morning and we'd go see Scott again. J.V. wanted to tell him the adoption paperwork had been filed, and it would be good for them to have more time together.

I got home around 11:30 and found a note on the galley counter. Bill had been called to a crime scene and he'd taken Buddy along. I dialed his cell and asked where he was.

"Powerhouse Gym on Broadway," he said.

"Is Buddy in your car?"

"Yeah."

"Who died?"

"You're not gonna like it."

I felt my stomach clench. "Tell me."

"The victim is Joshua Crafford, a registered sex offender."

"Knife wound?"

"Yeah."

"Garlic?"

"Yup."

"Shit."

"My thoughts exactly."

"Why don't I come and get Buddy out of your car. You'll be there a while, right?"

"Actually the body was discovered this morning. They called me after they did the autopsy. I wanted to look at the crime scene while it's still relatively fresh. I'll be home in half an hour. Buddy's fine."

I sat at the galley counter thinking about my list of potential victims. Crafford wasn't on my list, so either he wasn't registered in Redwood City or he didn't have convictions for habitual sexual abuse of children.

I didn't feel the same sense of urgency working this case as I had with other murder investigations. I felt no compassion for the victims, other than Gloria, and my client was in no danger from the killer. I looked at my watch and decided it wasn't too late to call Elizabeth. Since her trawler door had been closed all day, I dialed Jack's home number. He answered after two rings.

"Good evening, Nikki."

Of course Jack has caller ID.

"Hey, Jack. I hope I'm not interrupting anything. I kind of need to talk to Elizabeth. Is she awake?"

"She's right here. Hold on."

I heard the phone being handed off.

"Hi, sweetie! I miss you."

"I miss you too. Have you got a few minutes? I need a sounding board."

"Of course," she said to me. "I'll take this downstairs," she said to Jack.

After a minute she was back on the line and I heard Jack set the receiver in the cradle, I assumed, in his bedroom.

"What's up, honey?"

"I have a problem with that case I told you about."

"What's the problem?"

I told her how I was feeling about the killer I was hunting for Scott. That I was ambivalent about tracking down someone who might be doing the world a favor, and how that ambivalence made me feel guilty.

When I was finished, she said, "Wow. So, what do you plan to do if you catch this person?"

"I don't know. That's what's bothering me. Normally it isn't even a question."

"Yeah, but this is different. Of course, whoever is killing all these people is disturbed. They need help, but probably not the kind of help they'd get in prison."

We talked for forty minutes and although nothing was resolved, at the end of the conversation I felt better knowing someone understood how I felt.

Bill and Buddy walked in as I was hanging up the phone.

"Elizabeth says hi," I said.

"How is Elizabeth?"

"She misses me."

He smiled knowingly.

We talked about the case until almost 1:00, and then went to bed. I slept fitfully, interrupted by dreams I couldn't remember when I woke up, but that left me worried about the decisions I'd have to make if I *was* able to catch Gloria's killer.

CHAPTER 16

ON SUNDAY MORNING I DRANK an entire pot of coffee before going to the gym. My metabolism has slowed since I quit smoking. I'm having trouble waking up in the morning, and I'm eating more comfort food in an effort to suppress all the feelings I'm not used to dealing with. I'm also bitchier than usual.

I warmed up on the treadmill then hit the StairMaster, took an aerobics class, and finally did sit-ups, pushups, and used the free weights. By the time I was finished the endorphins had overcome the lack of sleep and I felt pretty good. I took a shower and talked with my friends in the locker room as I dried my hair and put on make-up.

I was at the office by 9:00. I called Bill

and asked him to bring Buddy up from the boat, then I called J.V. Trusty.

"How'd you sleep?" I asked.

"Kind of twitchy."

"Adoption nerves?"

"Yeah. How about you?"

"I didn't sleep much. I couldn't stop thinking."

"I'm not surprised. What are we doing today?"

"Whatever you want. Oh, by the way, another sex registrant was killed yesterday. I didn't find out until I got home last night."

"Jesus Christ," he said. "How many have there been?"

"Five, if you count Scott's mom."

"When was the first one?"

"October."

"Could be more than one killer working together."

"It's possible, but teams of multiple murderers are rare. Someone capable of this type of crime usually requires isolation."

"There have been exceptions. Remember the Chicago Rippers? Chris Worrell and James Miller, Leopold and Loeb. And what about the Menendez brothers? That might be what you're looking for. A pair of siblings who were sexually abused as children."

I didn't want there to be more than one killer. One was already more than I could deal with.

"Maybe," I hedged. "How about I borrow you a car and we spend the morning staking out potential victims, then go see Scott this afternoon."

"That works for me."

I called the Brewsters and spoke with Ilene before asking to speak with Scott. She was excited about the adoption and said we could come by and pick him up anytime. While I was waiting for Scott to come to the line I decided not to tell him what J.V. and I were doing that morning.

"Hi, Nikki."

"Hey. You want to get together this afternoon? Buddy and J.V. would like to spend some time with you."

"Sure. When?"

"Around two? If I eat any more Quarter Pounders I won't fit into my jeans."

"Okay." He sounded disappointed.

"Of course, you can have all the Quarter Pounders you want. Don't fill up at lunch and we'll stop at McDonald's after we pick you up. How does that sound?"

"Great!"

I hung up with a smile on my face.

Nancy Skopin

I called Elizabeth and talked her, and then Jack, into joining the stakeout. There were five potential victims on my list. This morning we would have four of them covered.

Bill walked into the office with Buddy, read the expression on my face and said, "What?"

"I need a favor," I began. "J.V. needs to borrow your car this morning."

"No. Absolutely not."

Bill drives a fire engine red, classic Mustang. It's totally cherry and no one else is allowed to drive it.

"Okay, you can lend me the Mustang and I'll give J.V. the BMW."

"Not on your life."

"Hey! I'm a good driver. I haven't gotten so much as a parking ticket in the last five years."

"That doesn't mean anything."

"Bill, J.V. needs a car. He's helping me with surveillance. Be reasonable."

"I'm not working today. I'll come with you."

This was Bill's idea of a compromise.

"Fine. Elizabeth and Jack will be here in ten minutes. I'll give them their subject files and then we'll go get Jack."

I looked through my stack of sex registrants and put them in sequence with the worst offender on the top, then I grabbed two bottles of spring water from the office fridge and stuffed them into my purse. Buddy gets thirsty during stakeouts.

Jack and Elizabeth arrived at 9:25. Jack is about five-ten, compact, and muscular. He's an Irishman with red hair sun-streaked with gold and green cat's eyes. His accent is only really obvious when he's annoyed.

I handed them printouts on the subjects they would be watching. I gave Pablo Morales to Jack and Timothy Vasey to Elizabeth. They silently read about the crimes committed by their subjects, looked at each other, and then looked at me.

"All you have to do is sit in your car, and watch." I looked at Elizabeth as I said this, wanting to be sure she heard me. "Even if you see someone suspicious approaching the subject, don't do anything. If one of them is attacked you can call nine-one-one and give a detailed description of the assailant, but do not approach them."

"Nikki," Elizabeth said, "I *have* done surveillance for you before."

"This killer is unpredictable."

"All killers are unpredictable. I'll be *fine.*"

I hugged her close and said, "Be careful," into her hair.

"I will, sweetie. Come have dinner with us at Jack's house tonight. Ilsa will make something wonderful."

Ilsa Richter is Jack's cook and house-keeper, and her husband Joachim tends to the grounds.

I glanced at Bill and he nodded. "Great," I said. "Can we bring J.V.?"

"Absolutely. We'd like to meet him. In fact, why don't you bring Scott too?"

"Scott has school tomorrow."

We locked up the office and hustled out to the parking lot. Buddy jumped into the Bimmer and whined when Bill got into his own car instead of riding with us. We motored up to Madison Avenue, where J.V. was waiting on Bill's front porch.

"I told Scott we'd be there at two," I said, "so that gives us four hours." I handed him the report on Gabriel Adamson.

J.V. studied the photo, and when he read the list of crimes sparks shot out of his eyes. *"Cocksucker,"* he hissed. He glanced at me. "Sorry, Nikki."

I tried not to laugh. J.V. had such a

cherubic face that it was hard to remember he was a tough-as-nails PI.

I removed my car key from the ring and handed it to him. "Keep your cell phone set on vibrate."

"Will do."

"You can follow us to Adamson's," I said. "We'll leave you there and head over to Tooker's hotel. Buddy's riding with you." I handed him a bottle of water. "If he gets thirsty, hook him to his leash and get him out of the car, pull the sports-top open on the bottle, turn it upside down, and squeeze gently. He's used to drinking from these."

"Good dog," said J.V., then to Bill, "Nice Mustang."

Bill beamed proudly and rested a hand on the hood of his car. "Thanks."

We caravanned off and I could see Buddy licking J.V.'s cheek in the rearview mirror. J.V. was laughing.

We pulled to the curb half a block from Adamson's address on 5th. I discreetly pointed out the dilapidated bungalow to J.V., got kisses from Buddy, and told him to be a good boy.

Tooker was staying in a hotel on Broadway in downtown Redwood City. We parked across the street and I dug around in my purse for my mini binoculars. After an hour I began to regret the last cup of coffee. Stakeouts are a bitch under the best of circumstances, but when you have to pee they're unbearable. I crossed and uncrossed my legs and squirmed around a lot, but eventually gave up.

"I need a bathroom," I told Bill. "Call my cell if he comes out." I handed him the binoculars and the photo of Tooker.

I hustled to a second-hand store on the corner, browsed a little, then picked up a small copper plate and paid cash for it, asking the cashier where the restroom was. She handed me a key chained to a hubcap and pointed toward the back of the store. I was just finishing up when my cell phone vibrated in my pocket. I returned the hubcap and answered my phone, power walking toward the door.

"He's on the move," Bill said.

"Which direction?"

"Headed toward Middlefield, on foot."

I was a block closer to Middlefield than Bill was. As I stepped outside I looked across the street and spotted a tall man with dark hair, three days growth of beard, and shifty eyes, walking toward the intersection of Middlefield and Broadway.

"I got him," I said.

I could guess where he was going. The public library had weekend story time events that drew crowds of children. I'd seen parents browsing the DVD section, thinking it was safe to leave their kids in the care of the reader. All Tooker would need was one child wandering away from the group. I picked up my pace as he turned the corner onto Middlefield.

"He's going to the library," I told Bill. "I think there's story time today. Where are you?"

"Right behind you."

I glanced over my shoulder as the Mustang passed me and turned into the library parking lot. Bill caught up with me at the front doors and we entered together, but split up once we were inside. He went to check out the men's restroom and I headed to the area where I'd seen children gathered in the past.

A woman wearing a fairy princess costume was setting up tiny folding chairs.

"What time does the reading start?" I asked.

"At eleven-thirty," she said.

Her voice sounded just like Glinda the

Good from the Wizard of Oz. Probably an affectation, but it gave me the creeps.

I scanned the area for Tooker. There was no sign of him. I went to the paperback racks and selected a mystery novel, then seated myself on the steps leading down to the children's books section and pretended to read. As an afterthought I slipped my cell phone out of my pocket and held it in my hand, ready to speed dial Bill.

Ten minutes later the kids started filing in. I wondered what Bill was up to. Maybe Tooker was in the men's room and Bill didn't want to leave him alone in case an unaccompanied boy wandered in. I shuddered at the thought.

By 11:35 all the chairs were occupied with kids between three and six, and Glinda announced the title of the book she would be reading. It was called *Stellaluna* and was about a baby fruit bat. She held up the book, showing the cover, and there was an excited twittering among the toddlers.

I looked around and counted only six moms and one dad present. There were at least twenty kids and only seven parents keeping an eye on them. Tooker could have a field day with these odds.

I settled in, resigned to hearing the fruit

bat story. Twenty minutes into the reading a little boy of about four got up and wandered away. None of the parents looked after him, so I followed. I called Bill's cell. I knew his phone was set on vibrate because it always is. He hates all the ring tone options. He picked up instantly.

"Are you still in the men's room?"

He texted me back saying, "Yes."

"Is Tooker in there?"

"Yes," Bill texted.

"I think there's a little boy on his way in."

He disconnected.

Since Tooker was in the men's room, I felt safe leaving the group of children for the moment. I scrambled between bookshelves and got to the restroom doorway right behind the toddler. I watched him go inside and held my breath. I didn't have long to wait. After a few seconds I heard a high-pitched scream, then some scuffling noises, and Bill pushed Tooker, face first, through the swinging door, his hands cuffed behind his back. Tooker's face was red and Bill's was etched in stone. He was quietly telling Tooker his rights. He broke off when he saw me.

"Go inside and make sure the kid's okay.

And find his parents. They'll need to bring him to the station."

"Okay."

I hesitated only an instant before pushing open the men's room door and peering inside. The little boy I'd followed was sitting in a puddle in the corner of the room, crying. His jeans were bunched around his knees.

I approached slowly and knelt in front of him. "Are you hurt?" I asked.

"Nnnooo," he wailed.

"Is your mommy or daddy here today?"

"Moooommmmmmmyyyy!" he cried.

"Okay, let's get you dressed."

I carefully pulled up his briefs and jeans, hoping not to disturb any evidence. I buttoned and zipped his pants and picked him up.

"My name is Nikki," I said. "What's yours?"

"Jake," he said, and wiped his nose with a balled fist.

"Hi, Jake," I said, stepping out of the restroom. "What's your last name?"

"Houser."

"Let's see if we can find your mom."

I walked to the front lobby and located

an employee who reluctantly agreed to page Jake's parents.

Moments later his mother appeared and snatched him out of my arms. "What's going on?" she demanded.

"Try to stay calm," I said. "Is your husband here with you?"

"No. Who are you?"

"Can we go outside?"

"Why? What happened to my son?" Jake was still sniffling, but he appeared to be interested in the conversation.

"I think we should go outside," I said again.

I took her by the arm and moved her toward the door, reaching into my bag for my ID. When we were on the sidewalk I held it up so she could read it without letting go of Jake, and said, "Ms. Houser, my name is Nicoli Hunter. I'm a PI and I'm working on a case that involves the surveillance of local sex registrants."

She physically withdrew from me as though saying the words made me one of them.

"I was here today with a Redwood City Police Detective, Bill Anderson. Detective Anderson was in the men's restroom covertly observing one of these registrants when your son entered the room. I'm afraid the suspect may have touched Jake in an inappropriate way before Detective Anderson apprehended him. The detective asked me to bring you and Jake to the police station."

I watched her eyes widen as I spoke. Finally she looked at her son. "Jakie, did the bad man hurt you?" Jake's little face flushed and he burrowed into his mom's shoulder. "You have to tell Momma. Come on." She leaned away from her son, studying his face, and her eyes filled with tears.

"I was trying to tinkle, and he grabbed me," Jake whispered.

I felt my stomach knotting up as Jake's mom held him close and they both dissolved into tears.

I let them cry it out, saying nothing, while I dug in my purse for a tissue. I came up with a crumpled but unused Kleenex and offered it to her. She took it gratefully, wiped her son's face and blew his nose.

"I need to call his father," she said.

"You can do that from the police station," I said, remembering I had no car. "May I ride with you?"

She hesitated a moment, searching my eyes before saying, "I guess so. I don't even know where the police station is. We live in Menlo Park."

"It's only a few blocks from here, on Maple. I'll give you directions."

Ms. Houser drove a silver Lexus SUV. She harnessed Jake into his safety seat in the back, and I climbed into the front seat next to her.

Apart from driving directions, there was no conversation on the way to the station. When we arrived I showed her where to park and then I called Bill.

"We're here," I said, when he answered. "What do you want us to do?"

"I'll come out," he said.

We waited a few minutes before Bill came down the front steps and approached the SUV. He held up his badge and Ms. Houser lowered her window. I made the introductions.

Bill explained what he had witnessed, told her that the suspect was in custody, and that he needed to interview Jake. He said nothing about an examination by a physician, but I guessed that was coming. He just didn't want to spook her. Bill works crimes against persons also known as body crimes, which include homicide, robbery, assault, and sex crimes. He'd done this before and I'd heard some of the details when he needed to vent.

After a brief conversation, Ms. Houser climbed out of the car and unstrapped Jake from his seat. She beeped the car locked, and carried him inside. I followed at a distance, not sure how I could help. Bill escorted her into an interview room and turned to me before going inside.

"She hasn't called her husband yet," I whispered.

"It's better to get the statement immediately after the event," he said. "You mind waiting out here?"

"No, of course not."

I sat down on a sectional in the hallway and tried to breathe as I imagined what Jake's mom must be going through. Then I remembered Scott and checked my watch. It was 12:20. There was still plenty of time before we were scheduled to pick him up. I wondered how J.V. and Buddy were doing with their stakeout.

Bill spoke with Jake and his mom for half an hour, then he left them in the interview room and came out into the hall.

"I need to set up an exam for Jake at the hospital," he said.

I followed Bill through the bullpen maze

and listened as he called the doctor and explained the situation.

"The contact was minimal," he said, "and I don't want to further traumatize the kid, so talk to him about what you're doing when you examine him. And talk to his mom. She'll want to be present. Yeah, okay. I'll bring them right over."

I knew Bill was upset by what was happening to Jake and his family. I didn't know what to say, so I just leaned in for a hug.

"I need to stay with them," he said. "Sorry."

"Don't be sorry. I hate to think what might have happened if you hadn't been there."

"Try not to think about it," he said. "I'll have someone drive you home."

"I can walk. It's less than a mile."

"Okay. I'll call you later."

"Call me on my cell. J.V. and I will be with Scott after two, and remember we're having dinner with Elizabeth and Jack tonight."

"Right."

Bill escorted me to the lobby and gave me a quick kiss before going back inside. I didn't envy him his job on days like this, but I was glad there was someone like him doing it.

Walking back to the marina I craved a cigarette more powerfully than I had since I first quit. This was the kind of situation I did not want to experience without the benefit of nicotine. I wondered what Bill did with his feelings. I knew he was a passionate man, but in the five months we'd known each other I'd never seen him cry. He seldom lost his temper. He didn't drink heavily. Maybe sex was his drug of choice. I could live with that.

J.V. had agreed to meet me at the office at 1:30, so I didn't bother calling him when I arrived. I sat at my desk drinking a cold bottle of spring water, trying to distance myself from the events of the day.

At 1:25 Buddy dragged J.V. into the office. Buddy pounced into my lap and J.V. dropped the leash and lit a cigar. His eyes were bright with excitement.

I took an ashtray out of a drawer and set it on top of my desk.

"We need to get going pretty soon if we're picking Scott up at two," he said.

"Any action from Adamson?" I asked.

"Son of a bitch went to church," he said. "Celebration Fellowship, right there on Fifth. I followed him inside, thinking maybe he got religion in prison, but it turns out they have a daycare center that operates during church services. He hung out in the hallway watching the kids through a glass pane in the wall. I stayed with him. None of the kids left the room, so he didn't have an opportunity. What about the guy you were tailing?"

"Grabbed a four-year-old boy in the men's room at the public library. Bill was waiting in one of the stalls and busted him on the spot. You have another one of those cigars?"

He withdrew a box of Old Port rum-flavored cigars from his pocket and shook one out of the package. I inhaled the fragrance as I unwrapped it. J.V. produced a lighter and offered me the flame.

I inhaled deeply, coughed once, and sighed. "God, I miss smoking."

Buddy wrinkled his nose and went looking for his water dish. After he'd had a long drink I put out the cigar and locked up the office. As we walked to the parking lot J.V. handed me the car key. He had parked the BMW in the fire lane. I let Buddy into the back seat and opened the vent windows for him.

"I took him for a walk while I was waiting for Adamson to come out of his house," J.V. said. "And we walked around a little out here before going to your office. He should be okay for a couple of hours at least."

"What a good boy," I said, ruffling the pup's ears.

CHAPTER 17

TRAFFIC WAS HEAVY FOR A Sunday and the drive to Burlingame took longer than usual, so we pulled up in front of the Brewster's house a little after 2:00. Before we were even out of the car, Scott was out the front door and halfway down the walk. Buddy chuffed out a whisper-bark, and Scott reached in through the open vent and gave him a pat, then turned to J.V.

"How are you doin' today, young man?" J.V. asked.

"I'm fine, sir."

This was way too formal. I needed to get these two to relax around each other.

We stopped at McDonald's and got Scott a Quarter Pounder. I ordered a Southwest Salad with grilled chicken and J.V. got an Artisan Grilled Chicken Sandwich.

It had started drizzling so we decided to eat in the car. I scanned my memory for something fun do to on a rainy day.

"Hey, Scott, have you ever been to the Exploratorium?"

"What's that?"

"Do you like science?"

"Science is cool."

"The Exploratorium is a big building filled with hundreds of science experiments that you can play with. It's in San Francisco. You guys wanna go?"

The decision was unanimous, so we took off for San Francisco. While we were on the road, J.V. told Scott that he'd filed the adoption application, and they talked about the waiting period. J.V. had asked them to put a rush on the process, which meant that if they were lucky they'd be able to spend the holidays together as a family. Because it was an interstate adoption, when he got back to Seattle J.V. would be required to take a physical exam and be fingerprinted by the ICPC. There would also be a home study interview to ensure his house was suitable for a child. Scott would be interviewed by the San Mateo County branch of Child and Family Services, to make sure he was comfortable with J.V. When all of that was done, Scott would be placed with J.V. for six months, and a social worker in Seattle would conduct monthly visits to see how Scott was doing in school and how the relationship was developing. After six months, providing everything was going well, the adoption would be finalized.

J.V. navigated using the GPS on his cell, and I managed to locate Pier 15. I parked in the Embarcadero garage, and handed J.V. my umbrella, saying I wanted to walk Buddy before going inside.

"You better keep this, then," he said, handing the umbrella back. "We don't mind a little water, do we Scott?"

"I like the rain," Scott said.

I remembered J.V. telling Scott that it rained a lot in Seattle.

Buddy and I walked around the pier, sniffing planter boxes and watering lamp posts. I took a bottle of water out of my purse and gave him a drink. Back at the car I fed him the remnants of my chicken salad. He ate everything that had salad dressing on it, but rejected the unadorned lettuce. When I was satisfied that Buddy knew he was loved, I opened the windows enough for air circulation, and locked the car.

I paid the fourteen-dollar admission

fee and entered the cavernous building in search of my two charges. Of course they were nowhere to be found, so I went to the information desk and asked what the most popular exhibits were. The young woman behind the counter told me to check out Electricity and Magnetism. She gave me a map and pointed out the location.

On my journey toward the center of the building I passed the Exploratorium Store and couldn't resist a quick look around. I picked up a Star and Sphere Kit for Scott and bought Exploratorium logo tee shirts that would change color in the sunlight for all three of us.

I continued my hike through the facility, keeping my eyes peeled for J.V. and Scott, but I found myself scrutinizing the other adults, especially the ones who were alone. This case was changing the way I viewed the world, and not in a way that was enjoyable. Prior to this I'd had no idea how common sexual abuse of children had become. It had probably always been this prevalent and was just being reported more openly. I'd heard about it on the news, but I'd been naive enough to believe it wasn't happening so close to home.

I finally found Scott and J.V. coming out

of the *Seeing* exhibit, talking enthusiastically about the difference between what they thought they had seen and what had actually happened. They'd watched a demonstration and then everyone in the exhibit was asked to recount what they had witnessed. Almost everyone had a different story.

We toured the other exhibits, stopping briefly at some and lingering at others. I kept quiet most of the time, letting the two of them get to know each other. By 5:15 my feet hurt and I was ready to call it a day. We walked across the street to the parking garage, and while J.V. and Scott walked Buddy I called Ilene Brewster.

"I'm afraid we kept Scott out longer than I had planned," I said. "We're at the Exploratorium. Have you fed the other kids dinner yet? We can stop somewhere before dropping Scott off."

"I'm just putting supper on the table," she said. "I'll keep a plate warm for Scottie."

"That's a good idea. You probably feed him vegetables. I've been filling him up with fast food."

The drive back to Burlingame was quiet. When I got off the freeway and stopped at a light, I turned and saw that both J.V. and Scott had fallen asleep. Scott was draped over

Buddy in the back seat and J.V. was propped up against the passenger side window, a soft smile on his face.

When I pulled to the curb in front of the Brewster's house I gave J.V. a gentle nudge.

He sputtered and said, "I was just resting my eyes."

Scott gave Buddy one last sleepy hug before getting out of the car with his Exploratorium gift bag, and J.V. and I walked him to the door.

"When will I see you again?" Scott asked J.V.

"I have to go back to Seattle so the adoption people can interview me, and they want to look at my house, but I can come back next weekend if you want."

"Okay."

Still half asleep, Scott wrapped his arms around J.V.'s waist and hugged him. When Ilene opened the door and Scott slipped inside, J.V. took off his glasses and swiped at his eyes.

We stood on the porch for a minute, filling Ilene in on the timing of the adoption process and J.V.'s plans for another visit next weekend.

On the way back to Redwood City I

asked J.V. if he wanted to work the stakeout with me again tomorrow.

"I booked a morning flight," he said. "I want to get the process started in Seattle. The Brewster woman seems nice, but Scott needs a real home. He needs stability. I have to pick out a school and get some kid-size furniture for his room."

"You've given this a lot of thought," I said.

"I always wanted kids. When we found out Roselyn couldn't have any, she didn't want to adopt. That just about broke my heart, but she was the love of my life, so I didn't let on."

"Better late than never," I said. "You up for dinner with Elizabeth and Jack tonight?"

"I think I'll get some sleep."

"What time is your flight?"

"Eight fifteen."

"I'll pick you up at six."

"No need for that. I can take a cab."

"It's no trouble. I'll be up anyway."

"Are you always this stubborn?"

"Pretty much."

"Well, so am I. I'll take a cab. Where should I leave the house key?"

"Why don't you hang on to it. You'll

need it next weekend." I was pretty sure Bill wouldn't object.

I dropped J.V. off at Bill's house and drove back to the marina.

CHAPTER 18

❦

BUDDY AND I BOARDED THE boat at 6:25 p.m. It was quiet and only a few lights were on inside. I normally leave all the lights on when I'm out at night. I hate coming home to a dark boat, but Bill has a problem with wasting electricity, so he turns them off when I'm not around. I hadn't seen his Mustang in the parking lot and wondered if he was still involved in this morning's bust.

I turned on the lights in the main salon and checked my voicemail. There was one message. Buddy and I listened as Bill explained that Tooker had hired a lawyer who was demanding a bail hearing tomorrow.

I called him back to confirm that he wouldn't be joining me at Jack's house for dinner. Then I fed Buddy some kibble and took a quick shower.

Jack McGuire lives in a Tudor mansion in Hillsborough. I'd discovered the property for sale while working on an investigation for Jack. I fell in love with the estate, and then Elizabeth fell in love with it, and then Jack fell in love with Elizabeth, so he bought the place. Have I mentioned that Jack is extremely well off?

Buddy and I pulled up to the security gate at 7:01. I was reaching for the intercom when the gate slid open. Someone had been watching for me. I tooled down the long driveway and pulled up in front of the main house where Jack and Elizabeth were waiting.

It had stopped raining and was a pleasantly cool evening. Buddy jumped out of the car and pranced over to Elizabeth who squatted down to give him a hug. He licked her face a couple of times, and then jumped up on Jack, resting his big paws on the Irishman's shoulders.

Jack and Elizabeth are a radiant couple. They're both beautiful, but they really shine in each other's presence. Seeing how happy they are together takes some of the sting out of how much I miss my best friend when she's staying with Jack instead of on her trawler at the marina.

Elizabeth reached up to hug me and Jack threw an arm around my shoulder.

"What's for dinner?" I asked. "I had salad for lunch and I'm starved."

Elizabeth said, "Ilsa knew you were coming, so she made low-fat lasagna. Where's Bill?"

"He's working. The guy we were tailing molested a little boy in the library men's room. Bill was hiding in a stall and caught him in the act."

"*Jesus Christ!*"

"I know. Where's K.C.?"

K.C. is Elizabeth's fifteen-pound orange tabby cat. I was worried about an encounter with Buddy. He seemed okay with the marina cats, but they mostly stayed out of his path.

"He's prowling around the grounds. Ilsa kept him inside all day while it was raining, so now he's out exploring."

We went into the house and Jack handed me a bottle of Guinness Stout while Elizabeth told me about the surveillance she had conducted that day. She had stayed with Vasey until late afternoon.

"He went to the Hillsdale mall and hung out at the Disney Store," she said. "Talked to a couple of kids, but didn't try to touch them. He's got this intensity thing going on. You can kind of see it in his photo, but it's more dramatic in person. I think he tries to intimidate kids into going with him. It's really creepy."

"What's he driving?" I asked.

"A rusty old Toyota pickup," she said. "Yellow and black."

Jack sat down next to me on the couch and I reached into his breast pocket for the pack of Turkish Ovals I knew would be there. "Do you mind?"

"Of course not. Didn't you quit?"

"Shut up and give me a light."

Jack lit my cigarette and said, "Morales went to the Target store on El Camino. Toy department. His specialty seems to be talking up single moms who have infants or toddlers. He got a phone number from one lovely señora. When she left the store I had a chat with her. She'll be changing her number tomorrow."

We discussed the case over lasagna, green salad, and zucchini. At the end of the evening Ilsa presented me with a Tupper of leftovers for Bill.

Buddy and I got home around 10:30 and when we boarded the boat I could hear TV sounds coming from the main salon. Bill came into the galley when he heard Buddy leap down the companionway. I knew from the look on his face that he was unhappy about the way things were going with Tooker.

I presented him with the lasagna and he popped the lid and inhaled the aroma. Bill and Jack have issues. Jack's a retired cat burglar and Bill's a cop, but Ilsa Richter's cooking transcends even the most extreme disparity. Bill grabbed a fork and wolfed down the cold lasagna.

I grabbed a Guinness from the fridge, sat down at the galley counter, and told Bill about Elizabeth and Jack's surveillance experiences. His eyes glowed with anger when I told him about Morales getting the young mother's phone number. He smiled when I told him Jack had spoken with her and she was having her number changed.

"She'll probably never shop at Target again either," I said.

"What's happening with J.V.," he asked.

"He's flying home tomorrow, but he's coming back next weekend. I told him to keep the key to your house. I hope that's okay."

"It's fine. I like him."

"Me too. More importantly, Scott trusts him."

$\mathcal{C}\!\!\sim\!\! \oplus \ominus\!\!\sim\!\!)$

On Monday morning my eyes opened before the alarm went off. Bill was snoring softly beside me. Buddy was on the foot of the bed and opened one eye when I sat up, then closed it again. I started the coffee maker before climbing into the shower.

I was on my second cup when the guitar music on the Dream Machine began playing. I heard Bill groan. I poured him a mug of coffee and handed it to him as he stumbled into the galley.

"Good morning, sunshine."

"Umph," he grumbled.

"Sleep okay?"

He took a sip. "Not really," he said. Bill is not a morning person.

I left Buddy on board and went to the gym for a quick workout. I used all the upper body machines and the free weights, then did pushups and sit-ups.

When I got back to the boat Bill had showered and dressed, and was feeding Buddy scrambled eggs with Canadian bacon chopped up in them.

"Is there any left for me?" I asked.

"In the pan."

I filled my plate and sat down at the galley counter.

"So what time is the bail hearing?"

"Nine o'clock."

"Will you call me after?"

"I'll try."

"I think I'll see what Jonathan Lewis is doing today."

Lewis was the only predator on my list that we hadn't covered yesterday.

Bill nodded and sipped his coffee.

At 8:20 Buddy and I walked up to shore and took a stroll around the complex before unlocking the office. I checked my e-mail and voicemail messages, then looked at the report I'd printed on Jonathan Franklin Lewis. He rented an apartment on 2nd Avenue. I knew the complex, but would need to locate his unit once we were there.

I examined his photograph. He was a forty-one year old Caucasian, six-one and two hundred and fifty pounds, with brown hair and brown eyes. Not a bad looking guy if you could overlook the creep-out factor.

I parked on the street near the tenement lot at 9:02, and hooked Buddy to his leash. We found a directory near the pool and located Lewis's apartment on the third floor. I walked Buddy up three flights of outdoor stairs. I could hear the TV through Lewis's window, so someone was probably home. I looked down at the pool. I'd be able to see the apartment clearly from there.

Buddy and I walked back down the stairs and parked ourselves in deck chairs facing Lewis's unit. Luckily it wasn't raining. There were just a few puffy clouds in an otherwise sunny sky.

Two hours later there was still no activity, which is often the case with this type of surveillance, but I was feeling anxious about not accomplishing anything on Scott's case. Of course we'd nailed Tooker, but there was a chance he'd be back on the street before nightfall. I wasn't so sure the killer didn't have the right idea. I mentally kicked myself for the thought, but it forced me to acknowledge my own inner vigilante.

At 11:30 my cell phone rang. I knew it would be Bill.

"He's out."

"*Shit*. When?"

"Fifteen minutes ago. He was charged with a 288(a), so his bail was set at a hundred thousand, but he used a bail bondsman. The good news is that his prior was for aggravated sexual assault. If he's convicted, he'll be eligible for life imprisonment under the sexual assault "one strike you're out" law. Where are you?"

"Over on Second Avenue. Maybe I'll swing by Tooker's hotel."

"Be careful."

Buddy and I hustled out to the street and piled into the BMW. We stopped at a Taco Bell for a low fat Burrito Supreme, then drove the short distance to Broadway. I found a parking space outside the secondhand store with a good view of the hotel entrance. If Tooker had left the courthouse on foot he was probably already home. I thought about checking with the front desk, but I didn't want to tip my hand in case the desk clerk and Tooker were friendly.

After we finished the burrito, Buddy and I took a walk around the neighborhood. He lifted his leg on a few trees and a fire hydrant, and I did some window shopping, keeping one eye on anyone going into or coming out of the hotel.

At 3:00 I decided I'd had enough and we drove back to the marina. We took an extended walk around the wildlife refuge across the street, and then went to the office.

I was getting behind on my bar and restaurant surveys, so I pulled out my master schedule and made a list of what I would need to accomplish in the next week.

CHAPTER 19

C⸺ ⸺

Nina Jezek had heard about Nicholas Tooker's arrest from a coworker. It was all the buzz how Anderson had caught him in the act. She wished she had been there instead.

She wanted to attend the bail hearing, but couldn't risk it. Anderson would be there and they'd met on more than one occasion. He would recognize her. Anderson was a good cop. In a different world she might have made a move on him, even though she'd heard he was dating a female PI, of all things. She drove to the courthouse and sat in the parking lot in her old black Celica. It was not a noticeable car. She would wait and see what happened. Maybe Tooker would get what he had coming after all.

At 11:17 Tooker strode outside. He walked from Marshall to Broadway and turned right, *heading toward downtown Redwood City. Nina started her engine and followed. She passed him on Broadway and parked a block ahead, assuming he was on his way to the hotel. She fumbled with her keys, pretending to lock the trunk, and waited for Tooker to walk past. Instead, he cut down an alley. Nina looked over her shoulder just in time to see him make the turn. She sprinted to the alley and saw Tooker go in the back door of a liquor store.*

Five minutes later he exited the store carrying a brown paper bag and a pack of generic cigarettes. He stood in the alley opening the pack, lit one, and took a deep drag.

There was no one else in the alley. She might never have a better opportunity. Nina started walking toward Tooker, and when she was only a few yards away she said, "I'm lost. Can you tell me where the CVS Pharmacy is?"

Tooker looked annoyed. He nodded back the way she had come. "It's the other side of the Caltrain station."

Nina glanced around to see if anyone was nearby, then withdrew the switchblade from her pocket, snapping it open as she stepped forward, and jamming the knife up under his ribs. Tooker sputtered and coughed, spraying blood all over her face. Realizing she must have nicked a lung, Nina quickly pushed him off the blade and turned away. She heard a bottle break as Tooker hit the ground. It probably wasn't uncommon for drunks to pass out in this alley.

Nina wiped her face with her sleeve as she hurried back to her car where she had a roll of paper towels. She scrubbed at her face with one hand as she started the engine. Pulling away from the curb, she glanced in the rearview mirror. There were flecks of blood on her eyelids. She blinked rapidly as she drove, hoping to expel Tooker's bodily fluids with her tears.

CHAPTER 20

I WAS PUTTING THE FINISHING TOUCHES
on my schedule for the week when my
phone rang. For some reason the sound
startled me, and I jumped.

"Hunter Investigations," I snapped.

"Tooker's dead," Bill said without
preamble.

"What?"

"His body was found in an alley between
Broadway and Brewster."

"Let me guess, knife wound, garlic on
the blade?"

"They haven't done the autopsy yet, but
I'm betting on it."

"I sat outside his hotel until three. I
guess he never made it home."

"Apparently not."

"I hate to ask, but how many people

could have known about his bail hearing, I mean outside of the department?"

"There's always the victim's family. I'll be talking to Jake's parents."

"I understand you have to do that, but if the same weapon was used it wasn't them."

"I know," he sighed. "Any employees of the PD or the DA's office would have known about the hearing, and anyone they spoke with about the case. Could be dozens of people. It's the kind of thing people talk about."

"He was just arrested yesterday. It's too fast. I think our killer might be a cop."

That went over like a lead balloon.

After a minute I said, "You still there?"

"I'm here."

"I know you don't like the idea, but it would explain the timing."

"Maybe. I have to go."

"Hang on a sec."

I pulled out a legal pad and made a quick list of the killings I was aware of. Novacek had been killed in October, in Redwood City. Fernandez had been killed in early November, in Sunnyvale. Zogg had been killed in mid-November, in San Mateo. Gloria Freedman had been killed on November 21st, in Redwood City. Crafford had been killed on Saturday December 5th, in Redwood City, and Tooker, today, December 7th, in Redwood City.

"There have been six killings so far," I said, "and four of them were in Redwood City. Bill..."

"Yeah, yeah," he said, "I get the point," and he hung up.

I set the receiver in the cradle and looked down at my list. If it was a cop, it was probably someone local. It could be anyone with the RCPD, the San Mateo County Sheriff's office, or the DA's office. There had to be a reason why four of the killings had taken place in Redwood City. I wondered how many of Bill's coworkers had been molested as children.

I called his cell, got his voicemail, and left a message. "You might want to put tails on Adamson, Vasey, Lewis, and Morales. I can cover one of them, but I'm getting behind on my surveys so I have limited time." What else could I say? He knew the killer was escalating and he knew how to do his job.

Buddy and I went to Michelino's in San Mateo and did an early dinner and bar survey. Buddy had to wait in the car of course, but he netted chicken Parmesan leftovers.

Then we went to the Bel Mateo Bowl and I surveyed the bar and bowled a couple of games. I like bowling, but it's more fun when you're with friends. Also I take issue with wearing someone else's shoes, even if they are routinely sprayed with disinfectant.

After bowling we drove to 231 Ellsworth and I did another dinner and bar survey. That was everything I'd scheduled for Monday. At 8:40 we drove back to the marina.

I walked Buddy before unlocking the office and when we went inside my voicemail light was blinking. The message was from Bill. All he said was, "Same knife."

I typed up the dinner, bar, and bowling surveys and e-mailed electronic copies off to my clients, along with invoices. Time to call it a night.

Buddy and I walked down to the dock, stopping for a lengthy visit with D'Artagnon before we continued on to my boat. Prior to Buddy entering my life, D'Artagnon had been my canine collaborator. He would always listen attentively when I had a problem I needed to work out. Tonight I was apprehensive about how quickly the killer was accelerating. One murder in October, three in November, and then two in the first week of December. Something had happened to cause the escalation and I wondered if it was Gloria Freedman's death. As far as I knew, Gloria was not a child molester. That might have been the trigger.

I considered what I already knew. Since the killer had targeted sex offenders who preyed on children, clearly he or she felt compelled to defend sexually abused children. If someone who was not a sex offender was murdered there could be a tremendous feeling of guilt. If the killer needed to be the 'good guy' and then killed someone who wasn't the right kind of 'bad guy', it might have pushed him, or her, over the edge. Gloria was a terrible mother, but if she had gotten counseling she might have straightened out.

Onboard the boat I opened a Guinness and settled in front of the TV. Buddy likes watching America's Funniest Videos because of the animal clips. I located the channel and sat back with him sprawled across my lap for some mindless entertainment.

By the time Bill called, Buddy and I were asleep on the pilothouse settee. I woke up when Buddy jumped off my lap at the sound of the phone. I glanced at my watch. It was 12:13 a.m.

"You work too much," I complained.

"IA's getting involved."

IA is short for Internal Affairs, which meant I wasn't alone in believing that someone within the department might be responsible for the killings. Bill wasn't happy about that, and I couldn't blame him. The police department is like a brotherhood, and no one wants to believe someone in their family could venture this far over the line.

"What about surveillance of potential victims?" I asked.

"You know we've had staffing cuts. There's no one available right now."

"Anything new come out of the autopsy?"

"Tooker was HIV positive and there was an interruption in the blood spatter at the scene, which means some of the blood sprayed onto the killer. We got a partial shoe outline. Our killer has small feet. Could be a woman."

"Will that be common knowledge within the department?"

"People talk."

"How long does it take after exposure for the antibodies to show up in a blood test?"

"Couple of weeks, I think."

"Maybe the killer will use their medical insurance for an HIV test."

"That would be careless."

"Sometimes intelligent people behave reflexively under stress. Finding out you've been exposed to HIV has to be at the top of the stress-o-meter."

We ended the call and Buddy and I went to bed, but I couldn't stop thinking about how many child molesters were out there stalking innocent victims.

CHAPTER 21

F IRST THING TUESDAY MORNING I called
Jim Sutherland. Jim is a fellow PI and a
friend. We met when I was working my first
murder investigation. He was working for
the killer. Of course, he didn't know that at
the time.

"Superior Investigations," said a honeyed
female voice.

"Nikki Hunter calling for Jim."

"One moment please."

Jim picked up instantly. "Nikki! How's
it hangin'?"

"Low and to the left," I said. "I need
help with some daytime surveillance. Do
you have any free time?"

"Tell me about it."

I recounted the whole case for him and
when I was finished he said, "It might not

be the worst thing in the world to let sex offenders run around unprotected."

"I know what you mean, but I promised Scott I'd try to find out who killed his mom, so I have to do something."

"I can give you three or four hours tomorrow and Friday."

"I'll take it. Oh, I forgot to mention, there's no fee for this job."

Jim has a deep resonant laugh. When he stopped laughing he said, "How could I resist?"

Next I called Jack McGuire who said he could give me all the time I needed, and agreed to meet me at the office in thirty minutes.

Elizabeth works weekdays and I wasn't going to ask her to take time off from her job. I searched my memory for anyone else I could pull into this project.

I had four subjects to cover: Lewis, Adamson, Vasey, and Morales. I'd put Jack on Morales because he already knew what Morales looked like, where he lived, and what his pattern was. I'd put Jim with Adamson, because according to his file Adamson was dangerous and Jim was experienced. I'd take Lewis because he was an unknown. That left

Nancy Skopin

Vasey. Elizabeth had said Vasey liked the
Disney Store.

I picked up the phone and called my
friend, Lily. Lily is another boat dweller.
She's a freelance hardware engineer, so
her time is her own. She's also a post-
surgical transsexual. Lily had never worked
surveillance for me, but she has a high IQ,
a working knowledge of psychology, and is
indomitable, so I figured she'd be good at it.

"Hello, Nikki."

"Hi, Lily. You working on anything
important? I need help with a stakeout."

"Sounds more interesting than what I'm
doing now. Are you in the office?"

"Yes."

"I'll be right up."

Five minutes later her broad-shouldered
frame filled my doorway. Buddy greeted
Lily with hand licks, and she ruffled his ears
before sitting down across from me.

"You want coffee?" I asked.

"No thanks."

I told her about Scott and his mom, and
what had happened in the last week. She
listened without expression. It takes a lot
to shock Lily. When I said I needed her to
watch a guy who spent time at the Disney
Store she grinned and said, "I'll fit right in."

176

"Maybe you're right. You can follow Lewis instead if you want."

I pulled out the files I'd printed on Vasey and Lewis and handed them over. She read every word, muttering under her breath, and handed me back the Lewis file.

"Disney is fine," she said. "I'll dress conservatively and wear the Hillary wig."

Even dressed conservatively Lily stands out in a crowd, but if Vasey tried anything her former experience as a linebacker would come in handy.

"Elizabeth says he's driving a yellow and black Toyota pickup. Call me if anything happens."

I made sure she had my smartphone number programmed into her cell.

"Keep yours set on vibrate, in case I need to reach you."

"Will do. I'll go change and get right on this asshole."

Lily was walking out the door as Jack McGuire was coming in and they stopped to hug each other. Lily and Elizabeth went to school together and have remained close over the years. Any friend of Elizabeth's is important to Jack, which is heartwarming. Still, the hug was a humorous spectacle. Jack is about five-ten and all male, and Lily, in her heels, is around six-two and mostly female, except for the Adams apple and the shoulders.

Lily went on her way and Jack came inside. He looked at my face and offered me his pack of Turkish Ovals. I considered for only an instant before accepting.

"Thank you. Have a seat."

I told Jack about the most recent murder and the details of the crime scene, indicating that the killer was either a small man or a woman. He was fine covering Morales again and said he'd check the residence first. If Morales wasn't home, he'd go to the Target on El Camino Real. I didn't ask how he'd know if Morales was home. Being a retired cat burglar, he has the skills of a magician with all kinds of locks.

We walked out to the parking lot together and got into our respective BMWs.

"Be careful, Nikki," he said.

"You too."

Buddy and I arrived at Lewis's apartment complex at 9:32. Since I didn't know if Lewis had a car, we did the listening outside the apartment door thing again, and once again I heard TV sounds. We walked back downstairs and sat by the pool. It was an overcast day, but at the moment it wasn't raining. I took the paperback out of my purse and read a paragraph, glanced up at the apartment, read another paragraph, and glanced up at the apartment again. At 10:47 the door opened and a man stepped outside.

I pulled the photo of Lewis from my bag to refresh my memory. It looked like the same guy to me, brown hair, Caucasian, six-one, two hundred and fifty pounds. I put on my sunglasses and pretended to read my book. When Lewis was almost to the street Buddy and I got up and walked casually toward my car.

Lewis got into a beat-up, red Chevy truck with a camper shell on the back. I've read about the favored vehicles of rapists and kidnappers, so the camper shell made sense to me.

I followed Lewis at a distance as he drove to El Camino Real and turned south. He got in the right lane as we approached the Stanford shopping center and took the exit. He drove clockwise around the complex and pulled into the parking structure across from Macy's. I found an open space in the next row.

I quickly lowered the windows for Buddy and locked the car, hustling to catch up with Lewis. Not that he was hard to spot, but if he entered a store out of my line of sight I might lose him. He skirted around Macy's and headed for the courtyard. I scanned the retail signage and guessed where he was going. The Discovery Channel Store.

I entered the store on Lewis's heels and covertly watched him evaluate the customers. He zeroed in on a little girl, curly blonde hair, maybe four or five, who was playing with a stuffed baby giraffe she'd taken from a display. She held the toy in her chubby hands and her face was lit up with wonder. A thirty-something blonde woman, whom I guessed was her mother, was standing a few yards away talking on her cell.

Lewis picked up a giraffe baby and knelt down near the little girl. "This one is my daughter's favorite too," he said in a soothing voice. "I have a little girl just your age. She lost her giraffe baby, so I'm here to buy her a new one."

Somehow I hadn't expected a sexual predator to be clever. In my mind they were all low-IQ dirtbags. The mother glanced at Lewis and smiled while continuing her cell phone conversation.

"Maybe your mommy will let me buy a giraffe baby for you too," said Lewis.

The little girl's eyes got wide and she

looked up at her mother who now had her back turned and was speaking in hushed tones into her cell.

I watched with morbid fascination as Lewis took the stuffed animal from the child, then reached for her hand. He moved swiftly toward the front of the store. I didn't think I could outrun him, so I placed myself in his path and took out my defense spray.

"Excuse me," I said loudly enough to draw attention, but not quite shouting. "Is that your little girl?"

I shook the pepper spray to activate it and held it where Lewis could see it.

The woman turned, startled to see that her daughter was not where she had left her. "Hey!" she shouted. She dropped her phone and ran toward little girl, who was still holding onto Lewis's hand. "Mandy, come to Mommy!"

Mandy looked up at Lewis and then at the giraffe babies in his hand, and the waterworks started. I looked into his eyes and read the impulse to grab the kid and run warring with the desire to avoid another arrest. Finally he let go of Mandy's hand as her mother snatched her up. Lewis dropped the stuffed toys and shouldered his way past me, almost knocking me down. He shot me a glare that told me he would remember my face.

I tried to get Mandy's mom to stick around while I called Bill, but she refused, so I asked for her name and phone number. She said she didn't want to get involved.

"Tell your husband a convicted sex offender attempted to kidnap Mandy today," I said. "See if he thinks you should inform the police." I gave her my card. "If you call me first, I'll meet you at the station when you make your statement."

I pulled Lewis's file from my purse and forced her to read about his convictions.

"I know this is inconvenient for you, but think what might have happened if he'd gotten her into his truck. If you do nothing, he'll be free to abduct other children."

She collected her cell phone from where she had dropped it and avoided making eye contact with me as she and Mandy left the store.

I spoke with the manager, a young woman in her late twenties with a crew cut and an eyebrow ring. I convinced her to bag the surveillance video for the police. This would be crucial evidence, especially if Mandy's parents opted not to press charges.

Since Lewis knew what I looked like

there was no point trying to tail him again. I doubted he'd take another risk today anyway. I kept my pepper spray at the ready and called Bill on my cell as I walked back to the parking structure. I described what had happened and told him the store manager was holding the security video. He said he'd speak to the DA about the attempted kidnapping and send someone to pick up the surveillance DVD.

When I got to the garage Lewis's truck was gone. I unlocked the BMW and gave Buddy a long hug, then I drove to Peninsula Liquors and bought myself a pack of American Spirit Organic cigarettes.

CHAPTER 22

WHEN BUDDY AND I ARRIVED back at the office I called Jack McGuire for a progress report on Morales. He was in his car and Morales was inside the Fanny Pack, a strip club in Redwood City.

"Did you go in?"

"For a moment. The dancer on stage looks about sixteen."

"What's he drinking?"

"Draft beer."

"Does he have a car?"

"No. He walked here."

"You know some of those dancers work upstairs between sets," I said. I'd spent time at the Fanny Pack during a previous investigation.

"What's your point?"

"He might be in there for a while."

"He's doesn't even have a job. I doubt he has enough cash for a nooner."

"He might be collecting unemployment or welfare. I hate for you to have to sit in your car waiting for him to come out."

"It's a very comfortable car. Besides, it's better than telling Elizabeth I spent the afternoon looking at naked women."

"I see your point. Keep me posted."

I called Lily and found out that Vasey was at Huddart Park in Woodside.

"I'm not dressed for this," she said. "I stand out like a sore thumb."

"I can be there in fifteen minutes. We need to switch subjects anyway." I told her what had happened with Lewis at the Discovery Channel Store.

"Son of a bitch," she said.

Buddy and I locked up the office and made the drive to Woodside. Lily was easy to spot. She was wearing her black Chanel suit with Via Spiga pumps and her Hillary wig—a little conspicuous.

She pointed Vasey out to me and I gave her the sheet on Lewis and told her where his apartment was in the complex on 2nd Avenue.

"He's a big guy and he's feeling frustrated after this morning, so be cautious."

Lily smiled serenely. "I think I can handle it."

She took off in her white Econoline van and Buddy and I strolled around the park watering shrubs, trees, and benches.

Vasey was a thirty-five-year-old Caucasian, six-feet tall and a hundred and eighty pounds, with light brown hair and blue eyes. He was dressed in a white polo shirt, khaki slacks, a red windbreaker and white athletic shoes. *The better to kidnap your child in,* I thought.

Since it was a weekday, kids over six were in school, so the children visiting the park with their parents were all toddlers. A couple of them approached Buddy as their moms or dads looked on. I hoped this wouldn't give Vasey ideas about getting a dog in order to attract children.

I was wearing my sunglasses, in spite of the cloudy sky, so I could watch Vasey without being obvious. He was watching me too. Elizabeth was right about this guy being intense. His eyes were practically boring holes into me, shifting manically from my face, to the dog, to the toddlers petting the dog. When the kids wandered away from Buddy, I selected a bench near the playground, sat down, and took out my book.

Vasey hovered near a merry-go-round, which was occupied by a little boy and a little girl. Luckily their mom was right there, spinning the contraption as they shrieked happily. He moved to an unoccupied swing set, seated himself awkwardly, and swayed a few feet off the ground. After a while a dark-haired boy climbed out of the sandbox and made a beeline for the swings. I looked around anxiously for a dark-haired parent, but I didn't see one. There was an older woman seated at a picnic table casually watching the little boy while knitting. I walked Buddy over to the table and sat down next to her.

"Is that your grandson?" I asked.

She slowly turned her bifocals in my direction. "What?"

"The little boy on the swing. Is he your grandson?" It wasn't a complex question.

"Why, yes. How did you know?"

Vasey was on his feet, pushing the toddler's swing.

"I don't have time to explain, but the man pushing your grandson on the swing is a convicted sex offender. He hurts children.

187

I need your permission to get your grandson away from him. Any objection?"

"Oh my dear lord, *Jimmy!*" she screeched.

"Please, don't alarm Jimmy. I'll go get him."

Buddy and I approached as Vasey continued to push the swing.

Jimmy giggled and shouted, "Higher!"

When we got close I could see the sheen of sweat on Vasey's face. His compulsion was working him and Jimmy was dangerously close to becoming a statistic. For the second time that day I withdrew the defense spray from my purse and gave it a shake. There was a strong breeze and it was coming my way, so if I was going to hit Vasey with the spray I'd have to get upwind of him first. I'd also have to make sure Buddy was behind me when I squirted the noxious liquid, so he didn't catch the fallout.

When I was a few feet away from Vasey I said, "Okay, Jimmy. Grandma says it's time to go."

Vasey's head whipped around, his eyes dilated with anticipation, his lips parted in an aroused sneer. While he was looking at me, Jimmy swung back and hit him hard in the chest. The kid didn't weigh more than thirty pounds, but Vasey wasn't braced and the impact knocked him off balance. As he struggled to regain his footing I snatched Jimmy off the swing and headed toward Grandma.

"*Hey,*" Jimmy squealed.

Vasey made a lunge for the boy and I pivoted out of his reach as Buddy leaped into the air and clamped his teeth on Vasey's wrist.

"Call nine-one-one," I shouted at no one in particular.

Jimmy's grandma was on her feet, brandishing a knitting needle. "Get away from my grandson, you prick!"

I handed Jimmy over to his grandmother and turned on Vasey, who was trying to disengage himself from Buddy. The jacket kept Buddy's teeth from penetrating his flesh, but he wasn't letting go and I was afraid Vasey would hurt him, so I tugged on the leash and said, "Buddy, drop it!" He responded by growling deep in his throat, but did not loosen his grip. "Buddy, let go *now.*"

Vasey twisted his arm, Buddy released him, and he staggered backward.

"I'll sue!" He snarled.

"I'd like to see you try," I hissed. I shortened the leash as Buddy strained to get back at Vasey. "I know who you are, and I know what you do for kicks. I'll be reporting this to the police."

Vasey glared at me menacingly, looked down at my slavering eighty-five pound pup, and took off running.

I turned back to Jimmy and his grandmother. "Everybody okay?" I asked.

Grandma had Jimmy in a bear hug, still holding the knitting needle in case she needed to defend him. "We're fine. Thank you, young lady. I'm indebted to you."

I took out my cell and called Bill's office number. "Would you be willing to make a statement to the police about what happened here?" I asked, as my call rolled into voicemail.

"I most certainly would," she said. Feisty.

I left Bill an abbreviated message, then called his cell.

"Anderson."

"It's Nikki. I've been watching Vasey and he just made a move on a little boy in Huddart Park. Can you send someone to take a statement from the boy's grandmother?"

"I'll come myself," he said.

I knew Woodside wasn't technically Bill's jurisdiction, but he'd probably call the San Mateo County Sheriff's Department from his car.

"I'll wait here," I said.

After we hung up I tried to calm Jimmy's grandma, explaining that I was a PI working on an investigation that required me to follow registered sex offenders.

"My goodness. That's a dangerous line of work for a young woman. You must be very brave."

I didn't bother to tell her that more than thirty percent of PIs were women. I didn't want her to go into information overload.

"It's not always dangerous," I said. "This is an unusual case."

Bill arrived five minutes later in an unmarked car, and a Sheriff's department cruiser pulled into the lot behind him. I waved them over as Buddy began spinning on the lawn, wrapping his leash around my legs. He'd caught Bill's scent and was doing his happy dance.

After I'd given my statement and was on my way back to the marina, I realized I was exhausted.

Buddy and I went to the office and brewed a pot of coffee. I looked over my schedule for the week, moving things around so I wouldn't have to do any surveys that night. I needed a break.

I took out the cigarettes I'd purchased

earlier and lit one, inhaled deeply, and felt the nicotine kick-in. I was tempted to have a shot of tequila with my cigarette. I opened the Pendaflex drawer where I keep the liquor, and my phone rang. Saved by the bell.

"Hunter Investigations."

"Hi, Nikki." It was Scott.

"Hey, how are you doing?"

"I'm okay."

I glanced at my watch. "Are you calling from home?"

"I'm on the school bus."

"So, what do you think of your uncle?"

"He's cool, you know, for an old guy."

"He likes you too."

There was a moment of silence before he said, "What's happening with the investigation?"

So this was a business call. I wondered how much I should tell him. He was my client, but he was also a nine-year old boy, albeit a very mature one.

"One of the subjects we were following got murdered when no one was watching him," I began. "We think the killer might be a woman." He didn't need to know that I suspected the killer was also a cop.

"Was it one of those guys who hurts kids?"

"Yeah, it was."

"That's okay, then."

I didn't know what to say to that. I agreed with him, but I didn't want to admit it.

"It's still wrong," I said.

"How's Buddy?" Much more comfortable subject.

"Buddy is a very good dog. He helped me save a little boy today." I told him an abbreviated version of what had happened in Huddart Park.

After Scott and I hung up, I called Lily. She said Lewis had shown up at home around 1:15, was inside the apartment for half an hour, and then drove to the library. He'd gone to the reference section, seated himself at one of the public access computers and logged onto MySpace, an internet chat room frequented by preteens.

"Bill's trying to get a warrant. I'll tell him where you are. If Lewis moves, call me back."

I dialed Bill and told him Lewis was at the library. He already had the warrant. I told him to look for Lily and she would point Lewis out. I have to admit it was exhilarating, knowing one of these guys would be locked up, even for a little while.

I called Jack McGuire. He was still with

Morales, who was now at the Kmart on Veterans Boulevard.

"You think Elizabeth would like a stuffed panda?" he asked.

"Elizabeth loves stuffed animals. If she doesn't already have a panda you should definitely buy her one. The bigger the better."

"That's what I thought," he said.

"So what's Morales up to?"

"Same as before. He's hanging out in the toy department, flirting with pretty young mothers with toddlers in their carts."

I gave him Bill's cell number and said, "If he does anything illegal give Bill a call."

"If he does anything illegal I'll detain him and call you. You can call Bill. Bill doesn't like me very much."

"That's not entirely true. He just doesn't like what you used to do for a living."

"If you say so."

"Thank you, Jack. I owe you big time."

"You will never owe me, Nikki, and we both know why."

I recalled the case that had brought us together and flinched at the memory.

I opened the bottle of Jose Cuervo Especial and poured half a shot into my coffee. Then I called J.V. Trusty.

"Hello, Nicoli."

"Hi, J.V. What's new?"

"I'm furniture shopping," he said. "What do you think about bunk beds? I'm getting two twin over twin bunk beds."

"I think if you're nine years old there's nothing better."

"I want Scott to be able to invite his friends overnight on the weekends. See? You think two bunk beds will be enough?"

I tried not to laugh. "Two should be plenty."

"I got a nice little desk and some bookshelves. Maybe I'll get him a bicycle."

"Scott might like to pick that out himself."

"And sheets. I've got Spiderman sheets, Incredible Hulk sheets, and Fantastic Four sheets. It's all comin' together! I gotta tell you, Nikki, I'm having the time of my life."

"I'm glad."

"I even got him his own iPhone so he can call me any time he wants."

"Excellent. So when's the physical?"

"Tomorrow morning. They're coming to check out my house on Thursday."

"Have you booked your flight for this weekend yet?"

"Yes. I'm on the same flight as last time. Nine fifty-three Saturday morning."

"I'll meet you at baggage claim."

"Thank you, Nicoli."

I hung up the phone, sat back in my ergonomic swivel chair, and sipped the tequila laced coffee. Even if I never caught the person who had killed his mom, I knew Scott would have a good life with J.V.

CHAPTER 23

$\mathcal{C}_{\mathcal{Q}}$ $\mathcal{Q}_{\mathcal{Q}}$

NINA'S MOUTH WENT DRY AS she stared at the copy of Nicholas Tooker's autopsy report. She'd known there were risks and had been willing to take them, but this wasn't the kind of threat she had envisioned. She'd thought she might get caught and spend the rest of her life in prison. That she could handle. Contracting AIDS was not something she had bargained for.

Tooker's blood had gotten into her eyes. She'd showered as soon as she got home, but it was probably too late. She'd wait a few weeks before going to a clinic for an HIV test. In the meantime, she would take out as many pedophiles as possible.

Her next target was Alfredo "The Tongue" Giordano. Giordano was not a child molester. In fact, his sexual proclivities were rather conventional, but he pandered to sexual deviants and among his clients were several wealthy pedophiles. Giordano imported children from other countries for the purpose of sexual exploitation.

Although he could afford to live in a more affluent community, Giordano preferred the privacy and anonymity of Woodside Hills. He had gotten his nickname one morning when he was walking downstairs in a sex-induced haze after a vigorous encounter with a young woman. The doorbell rang and his cat, startled by the early morning visitor, had dashed down the stairs, weaving between Giordano's legs and tripping him. He'd fallen down the remaining stairs, cracking his chin on the marble floor below. His companion had come out of the bedroom just in time to see the cat eating the severed tip of Giordano's tongue. The incident had left him with a permanent speech impediment.

Nina had read his file and was aware that the Feds had been after him for years, but he was connected, and he was careful. She intended to put an end to his good fortune and, before she killed him, she hoped to obtain his client list. If she did have HIV, she no longer had anything to lose.

Giordano's file contained a number of

photographs of young women entering and leaving his home in Woodside. Each of them appeared to be in her twenties, slender, and had short hair. Nina was thirty, but she didn't look her age and she had the requisite lack of curves. It shouldn't be too hard to wrangle an invitation to his house. Once she was alone with him the rest would be easy.

CHAPTER 24

I CHANGED INTO AN OLD PAIR of jeans
and my foul weather boots, and Buddy
and I went for a three mile hike around the
wildlife refuge. When we were both worn
out, we walked back down to the boat for
a late lunch. I wasn't in the mood to cook,
so I tossed a green salad together with a
can of tuna. Buddy ate some kibble while
I scarfed down my salad, offering him the
occasional bite.

Lily dropped by at 3:45, cruising on a
wave of adrenaline from the part she had
played in Lewis's arrest. I offered her a
Guinness and she sat at the galley counter
and told me every detail of the take down at
the library. Her enthusiasm was contagious
and by the end of the story I was charged
up enough to continue the investigation.

If nothing else, we were making the streets safer for children.

After Lily went home, Buddy and I stretched out on the settee in the main salon and took a nap. The nap was interrupted a little after 6:00, when Bill called, inviting himself over for dinner. A few minutes later Buddy heard his Mustang.

I grabbed my jacket and his leash, and let him drag me up to shore.

Bill was getting out of his car in the boat owner's lot when we reached the gate. I scanned the area for traffic. When I didn't see any I let go of the leash and Buddy thundered across the lawn, did a couple of rocking horse spins, and flung himself at Bill.

I felt a pleasant clench in my chest as I watched them greet each other. They both added so much to my life. I'd spent years avoiding this kind of connection because of my fear of vulnerability. Now it was hard to imagine a future without both of them in it.

Over dinner, Bill told me the DA had charged Lewis with attempted kidnapping. His parole had been revoked, and bail would not be granted. Because attempted kidnapping was on the list of serious felonies included in California's three strikes statute, and because Lewis had two prior convictions, the DA was asking for a life sentence without the possibility of parole.

We cuddled in front of the TV after supper, trying to take our minds off the day's events.

That night my sleep was interrupted by dreams of toddlers being abducted. When I woke up in the middle of the night I tried to comfort myself with the knowledge that I was making a difference. I couldn't help wondering if the killer felt the same way.

Jim Sutherland met me at my office at 9:00 on Wednesday morning. Jim is just over six feet tall and solidly built, with red hair and a ruddy complexion. Three of my closest friends, Elizabeth, Jack, and Jim, are redheads. There's a famous quote by Mark Twain: "While the rest of the human race are descended from monkeys, redheads derive from cats." That certainly applies to Jack McGuire, whose facial features actually resemble those of a cat.

After he had properly greeted Buddy, I offered Jim coffee. He gratefully accepted, having worked late the previous night.

I had planned to put Jim on Adamson,

but after the attempted abduction in the park I decided to send him after Vasey, who would now recognize me. Bill had said the DA didn't think there was enough for a warrant to arrest Vasey yet.

I gave Jim the printout and described what had happened the day before. He grimaced when I told him about the little boy on the swing set. Jim has not been hardened by the years he's spent working as a PI.

When he left I called Jack and asked him to cover Adamson while I took Morales. He'd already spent two days shadowing Morales and I didn't want his face to become familiar.

Jack showed up at 9:35 and we went over Gabriel Adamson's file together. I described Adamson's bungalow on 5th Avenue and mentioned that on Sunday J.V. had followed him into a local church that housed a daycare center. I would be working in the same neighborhood today. Morales lived on Kramer Lane near 5th.

We left the office together, and Buddy and I picked Morales up outside his apartment complex shortly after ten o'clock. He was five-seven and a hundred and forty pounds, in his early thirties, with short black hair and a mustache. His nose looked like it had been broken at least once, but other than that he had a pretty, almost feminine face. He was dressed in jeans and a black sweater.

Morales was on foot so I hooked Buddy to his leash and locked up the Bimmer. I don't like tailing subjects on foot. It makes me self-conscious. Having Buddy along made me less conspicuous, but I worried that if there was a confrontation between myself and Morales, Buddy might get hurt. Of course, I could have left him in the car, but he hates being left alone and I didn't need the guilt.

Half a block from Morales's apartment I realized I'd be stuck if he went into a store or a bar that didn't allow dogs. Being an overprotective parent, I would never leave Buddy tied up outside such an establishment. Now I had a choice to make. I could hotfoot it back to my car and lock Buddy inside where he'd be safe albeit unhappy, or I could risk having Morales killed. I decided I didn't care that much if Morales bit the big one on my watch. If he went into a store or back to the Fanny Pack, I'd keep track of anyone who followed him inside and watch for blood spatter when the following subject came out again.

"It's a good plan," I said to Buddy, trying to convince myself.

Morales walked at a leisurely pace from Kramer to 5th, heading toward El Camino Real. We followed him past Jack McGuire's black BMW, which was parked on 5th a block from Vasey's cottage. I gave Jack a little wave as Buddy and I strolled by.

Morales turned north on El Camino and I thought, *Fanny Pack*. I wondered if Frank, the bartender I'd met on a previous case, still worked there. If so, he might let me bring Buddy inside with me.

Morales wasn't going to molest any children at the Fanny Pack. The women who worked there were beyond the age of consent, although some of them looked like teenagers. I was guessing those were the ones who interested Morales. It occurred to me that Alfred Miner, the owner of the Fanny Pack, would not be above employing underage girls to work upstairs, if not on the dance floor. I had to remind myself why I was following Morales. I was looking for someone who might want to kill him.

Buddy and I walked along El Camino Real, breathing exhaust fumes and enjoying the cool, but sunny, weather. A block from the Fanny Pack Morales turned into an adult bookstore. They'd probably let me bring the dog inside, but I didn't want to be noticed. I hadn't seen anyone else tailing Morales, so I skulked around the parking lot, trying to be invisible. A few minutes later Morales came out carrying a brown paper bag that appeared to contain a magazine or two. Reading material.

He walked the remaining distance to the Fanny Pack and went inside. Buddy and I huddled under a tree at the corner of the building. I lit a cigarette and watched as three other men entered, two together, one alone. I took a mental picture of the guy who went in alone. He was short and his feet looked small enough to match the print found in the alley where Tooker had been killed. I put out my cigarette, shortened Buddy's leash, and walked him inside.

The Fanny Pack had not changed in the months since I'd last visited. It was dark, the music was bone-jarring, and the air smelled of tobacco, beer, and human sweat. Although there were *No Smoking* signs posted at the entrance, the customers and employees chose to ignore the ordinance.

There was no doorman on duty at the moment, so I walked Buddy to the bar and hopped up on a stool. Frank Waters looked at me for a long moment before recognition kicked in. "Hey, the PI! Where's your friend Lisa?"

Elizabeth had come with me to the Fanny Pack once, and had given Frank a false name. He'd instantly developed a crush on her.

"She's engaged," I said. His face fell. "Sorry, Frank. Is it okay for me to have my dog in here?"

He leaned over the bar and looked down at the wagging pup. "I guess, as long as he doesn't come behind the bar. You want coffee?"

"Please."

While Frank filled a glass mug I looked around at the occupied tables. Morales was seated near the dance floor, smiling up at a gyrating blonde on the platform. He had some dollar bills in one hand and a draft beer in the other. I continued my scan of the room and spotted the man who had followed him in. The guy was getting a lap dance. Probably not the killer.

I spent almost an hour watching the door and trying not to watch the dancers. It was easy to keep tabs on Morales. He never left his seat. At 11:32 he stood up, adjusted himself, collected his paper bag, and headed for the door. Buddy and I waited a minute to see if anyone would follow. When no one did, I said goodbye to Frank and we hit the street.

Daylight is shocking when you've been in a semi-dark room for a prolonged period of time. I put on my sunglasses and spotted Morales heading north. Buddy and I followed him to a liquor store and a corner grocery, and then we followed him home where he reentered his apartment. We'd been on this guy's tail for almost three hours and he'd never once looked over his shoulder.

I'd had enough for the day, so we got into my car and drove back to the office. I'd been remiss in documenting what I was doing for Scott and at some point he might want an accounting. Even adolescent clients who pay very little have a right to regular reports.

I spent the early afternoon typing up notes on my activities, those of my friends, and the subjects we'd been tailing. When I was finished I had a fifty-three page document and a slight headache.

Buddy and I walked to The Diving Pelican and shared an order of Bennett's meatloaf.

After eating we went back to the office. I called Jim Sutherland and then Jack McGuire, but neither had anything of consequence to report. Vasey was window shopping at a Gymboree, and Adamson was at the Sequoia Station Barnes & Noble, hanging out in the children's books section. I asked Jack if Adamson had a car.

"He took the bus today," he said.

I hauled out my bar and restaurant schedule. I'd put off three surveys the previous night, which meant I'd have to do five tonight. I wondered if I could talk Elizabeth into coming along. I called her at work.

"Hi, sweetie," she said. "What's up?"

"I need an escort for dinner and drinks tonight. Have you had lunch?"

"I was just unwrapping my sandwich."

"Put it back in the fridge. You'll want to be hungry."

"Okay. Where are we eating?"

"Dominic's, Behan's, Pisces, Kuleto's, and the Elephant Bar."

"Wow! I should have skipped breakfast too."

"Two of them are bars, so you only have to eat three dinners."

"That's a relief. I'll wear something stretchy. What time?"

"I'll pick you up at six."

I called Bill to ask if he could puppy-sit

tonight, then locked up the office and took Buddy down to the boat.

I showered and did the whole grooming ritual; hair gel, blow dryer, eye shadow, eyeliner, mascara, and lip gloss. Then I dressed in black jeans and a gray silk turtleneck sweater. I was putting on earrings when Bill arrived.

"Hey," I said. "Why didn't Buddy tell me you were home?"

"I left the Mustang at work. I'm driving an unmarked."

"Because…"

"Because the way this killer is escalating, I expect to be called to a crime scene any minute and I don't like showing up in my own car. It's too recognizable."

"Oh. Please don't leave Buddy home alone if you get a call."

"I'll take him with me if I have to go out."

"Thank you. I'll see you boys later."

I kissed Bill and hugged Buddy before putting on my leather jacket. I was looking forward to an evening with my best girlfriend.

CHAPTER 25

E LIZABETH HAD THE DOOR TO her trawler closed tonight, but as I climbed her dock steps she slid it open before I could even knock.

"Hi, honey."

"Hi. Are you ready to go?"

"Just let me get my coat. Come inside."

Jack was standing in the galley sipping Irish whiskey, neat.

"How was your afternoon?" I asked.

"Puzzling."

"How so?"

"It isn't logical for a pedophile to stalk toddlers at a Gymboree. It's a children's clothing store. The kids are rarely unattended."

"What's your point?"

"I think Vasey may know he's being watched."

"That would make sense after what happened at the park yesterday. Do you think he spotted you?"

"Unlikely. Maybe he's just being cautious. I meant to ask you, this guy is on parole after doing time for child molestation, correct?"

"Yes."

"Aren't there conditions of parole that need to be met, like not hanging out in places that are heavily populated by children?"

"I don't know. If that's the case he's violating his parole all over the place."

"That's what I was thinking."

Elizabeth came back out wearing a calf length red cashmere coat and carrying a classic, red Coach duffle.

"Wow!" I said. "There are advantages to being engaged to a wealthy man."

"Wealth is only one of the many benefits of being with Jack," she said, giving him a kiss. "Did I tell you we set the date?"

"Already?"

"We've been engaged for almost two months! We decided on a year from next June 17th. It's a Saturday. Are you free?"

"I'll have to check my calendar. Of course I'm free, you idiot." It was a year and a half away, but I took out my smartphone and entered the date as we paraded up to shore. "Have you chosen a venue?"

"Hornblower Cruises hosts weddings aboard their yachts out of San Francisco. The ceremony would be performed by a uniformed captain. Then we could cruise around San Francisco Bay during the reception. It's just one possibility."

"That sounds perfect," I said.

I unlocked the 2002 and gave Jack a quick hug before he got into his own BMW and Elizabeth and I climbed into my car.

"By the way," she said, "Jack's going to ask you to be his best man."

"What?"

"He wants to ask you himself, but I thought you might need some time to think about it. You're his best friend in the states, besides me, of course."

"Will I have to wear a tux?"

"Not unless you want to."

"Who's going to be your maid of honor?"

"I thought I'd ask Lily."

"Oh my God. She'll flip!"

This was the kind of conversation I'd been missing. Bill is great to talk to, but he's a guy. I missed girl-talk.

We arrived at Dominic's and I allowed the valet to park my little 2002. It made me nervous, but Dominic's owner wanted his valets rated along with all the other employees. The young man was well groomed and polite, neatly dressed in black slacks, a white shirt, and a red jacket. He issued a receipt and thanked me before driving away, and he didn't screech my tires entering the parking lot. What more could you ask?

The service at Dominic's was excellent and all sales were properly recorded. Elizabeth and I took the opportunity to catch up on each other's lives while nibbling on risotto agli asparagi, which is a rice dish with herbs, wine, olive oil, and asparagus.

From Dominic's we moved on to Behan's, where we sipped light beer while evaluating the bartenders. Everything appeared to be in order, although one of the bar patrons was loud and obnoxious. As we were leaving I heard the female bartender ask him for his car keys. He started to protest, but she came out from behind the bar and deftly slipped her hand into his pocket, snatching away his keys.

"I'll call you a cab," she said. "Ride's on the house."

I wasn't sure if her proximity or the fact that her lacy bra was peeking out the top of her blouse quieted his objections, but he no longer seemed to mind. I enjoy adding this kind of detail to my reports.

At Pisces we both ordered the house salad and mineral water, causing our waiter to grimace reflexively. I made up for the stingy order with a healthy tip.

Our next stop was Kuleto's. Elizabeth ordered the chicken parmesan and I requested eggplant scaloppini. We shared our entrées, and both were scrumptious.

We ended the evening at the Elephant Bar over Irish cappuccinos. Since it was a weeknight and getting late, the crowd was thinning and we were able to have a conversation without shouting. I filled Elizabeth in on everything she didn't already know about Scott's case, and told her I was convinced the killer was a female who worked in law enforcement.

She said, "How can you hold a full time job and kill six people? What days of the week and times of day did the murders take place?"

I thought back over what Bill had told me.

"Gloria and Crafford were killed on Saturdays. The others were killed on different weekdays, and all during daylight hours, as far as I know."

"So you're looking for someone who calls in sick a lot, or who works nights."

"And who has strong feelings about protecting children."

"That should narrow it down some. Can you get a list of county employees and their work schedules?"

"I could ask Bill, but I doubt he'd be willing to help me with something like this. I'll have to think of another way."

When we arrived back at the marina I walked Elizabeth to the gate, then stopped by my office and typed up some quick notes to refresh my memory in the morning when I would complete the reports.

I shuffled down to the boat at 11:15, feeling overfed but satisfied by the lengthy visit with Elizabeth.

Bill and Buddy were waiting up for me. I presented them with three doggy bags and they tore through my leftovers with gusto.

While they were eating I asked, "Could there be any habitual sex offenders in the area who wouldn't be registered? Maybe someone who was arrested, but not convicted?"

Bill chewed and swallowed while nodding his head. "I assume you mean child molesters. There are several. The problem with this type of crime is that there are seldom witnesses, so we have to rely on the kids to tell us what happened. Kids are easily confused. They forget things, or get scared and change their story, so sometimes the DA won't prosecute." He sighed.

"You keep records of anyone who's been charged though, right?"

"Sure."

"Who has access to those?"

"Everyone in the records department, and all the detectives."

"Tell me about the records department. How many employees are there?"

"Day shift, there are three. Swing shift, only one."

Remembering my conversation with Elizabeth, I said, "Who's the swing shift employee?"

"Nina? She's a peach. Quiet, keeps to herself, very accurate."

"A peach?" I felt a stirring of jealousy. "Is she an attractive peach?"

"Babe, you are the only produce I'm interested in."

"Uh huh. So what's Nina's last name?"

"I don't remember. I've only met her a couple of times. Something Slavic I think."

"Can you find out? Maybe get me a social security number?"

He raised an eyebrow. "I told you IA's looking into this. Besides, you know I can't give you confidential information about RCPD employees."

"What if she's the killer?"

"Too timid." He continued stuffing his face.

"Can you at least get me a picture of her?"

"Nikki, stop. Nina is not a killer."

I went up on deck in a huff, lit a cigarette, and tried to mellow out. Bill's a good cop, but he's not objective when it comes to his coworkers. I wanted to look into this Nina person. Maybe I'd go hang out in front of the police station some afternoon and wait for her to arrive. Of course, she'd be parking in the secure lot. I could pretend to have a flat tire and flag her down, asking to use her cell phone. Maybe have Elizabeth hiding nearby with a camera. That would at least net me her license plate number, but I'd need someone besides Bill to run the plate through the DMV database. Then I remembered my friend Michael—an untapped resource. My childhood sweetheart, Michael Burke, is a white hat hacker, employed by Fortune 500 companies to test their network security. He could easily get into the DMV database and use Nina's plate number to obtain her driver's license number. Then I could run a background check.

CHAPTER 26

On Thursday morning I called Elizabeth first thing and she agreed to be my hidden cameraperson that afternoon. Bill had said Nina worked the swing shift, which is normally from 4:00 p.m. to 12:00 a.m., so Elizabeth would need to leave work early.

Bill was likely to be at the RCPD at 4:00, and if he caught me and Elizabeth in front of the building with a bogus flat tire, I was toast. So I'd have to think of a better plan. Maybe we could conceal ourselves in the bushes and take pictures of the license plates of every car entering the secure lot between 3:30 and 4:30. That might work, but I'd have to find someone to babysit Buddy. He's no good at hiding in the bushes.

He likes to play in the bushes. I thought of Jack McGuire.

Ilsa answered Jack's phone after two rings. "McGuire residence."

"Hi, Ilsa. This is Nicoli Hunter."

"Hello, Miss Hunter. How are you today?"

"I'm well, Ilsa. How are you doing?"

This kind of pleasantry is imperative with Ilsa Richter. If I were to call and just ask for Jack, she would feel slighted. After a brief discussion of her husband Joachim's health, she asked if I wanted to speak with Mister Jack.

"If he's available."

Moments later Jack picked up an extension. "What's up, Nikki?"

"I need a babysitter," I began. "Elizabeth and I are staking out the police department this afternoon and I can't bring Buddy. He's not good at hiding."

"No kidding. I'd be happy to sit with the boy. K.C. can hang out with Ilsa in the cottage."

"Thank you, Jack. I'll drop him off at 3:00."

It's great to have friends you can depend on.

I put a fresh battery into my Cyber-shot

mini camera, then typed up the dinner and bar surveys from the night before.

I was done by 11:30 and Buddy was prodding my leg with his nose, so I figured it was time for a walk. We strolled out to the point and watched the mallards frolic in the channel. Perhaps frolic is the wrong word. The mallards were mating. Mating is quite a production for ducks, and they aren't gentle about it. The male mounts the female from behind, grabbing onto the back of her neck, almost drowning her and pulling out clumps of feathers. There's a lot of quacking and squawking and thrashing about in the water. Buddy was fascinated.

We walked down to the boat and had kibble and yogurt for lunch. While we were eating I thought about J.V. Trusty and wondered how his physical had gone yesterday. Today they would be checking out his house. I made a mental note to call him and ask how the process was coming along.

At 2:40 I collected Buddy's favorite tennis ball and his stuffed dragon and chauffeured him to Jack's estate in Hillsborough. Buddy loves Jack. I watched the two of them playing fetch in the side yard while Joachim buzzed the gate closed behind me.

Elizabeth was waiting for me when I

arrived back at the marina. We ditched our purses in the office and grabbed my cameras. I carried the Nikon with a telephoto lens and handed her the Cyber-shot. We walked the short distance from the marina to the police department. As we approached the front of the building we skirted the parking area and ducked behind a large cluster of blooming bottlebrush. Not a good time to have pollen allergies. We positioned ourselves so that we had a view of the gate to the secure lot, focused our cameras, and waited.

Several cars drove out of the lot, but we ignored them. At 3:55 a black Celica pulled up to the gate. We started shooting pictures of the license plate as the driver's side window powered down. The engine shut off and a slender arm reached out the window. I noted a feminine profile beneath a large pair of sunglasses and felt a chill that was not provoked by the cool weather. The woman held a fob attached to her key ring up to the scanner and the security gate rolled open. I zoomed in on her face with my Nikon, snapping a few pictures before she started her engine, raised the window, and drove through the gate.

We stayed in place for another thirty minutes, taking photos of other cars and drivers, but the only other women to arrive were dressed in uniform. The driver of the Celica had to be Nina.

The sun was low in the sky when we arrived back at the marina. We retrieved our purses from the office and I followed Elizabeth's VW Beetle to Highway 101. When we arrived at the Hillsborough estate the gates swung open before she keyed in the security code and Jack and Buddy came out to greet us.

Watching the two of them with Buddy I wondered how long after the wedding Elizabeth and Jack planned to wait before having children. Elizabeth hadn't said anything, but I could see the writing on the wall. They'd make great parents, which is uncommon enough, but their love for each other would be passed on to the lucky offspring, and that was priceless.

I collected my dog and his toys, turning down the offer of dinner reluctantly. Buddy and I drove to the 1-Hour Photo in Redwood City and I dropped off the film from my Nikon. Then we went back to the office to check out the pictures Elizabeth had taken with the Cyber-shot.

The first picture of the license plate was fuzzy, but when I enlarged the second one I could make out the letters and numbers. I picked up the phone and called Michael Burke.

I got his voicemail and had started to leave a message for my reclusive friend when he picked up.

"Hello, Nikki."

"Screening your calls?"

"Naturally."

"Your number is unlisted. Who could be calling?"

"You never know."

"I need a favor. Can you run a license plate through the DMV database and get me a name and driver's license number?"

"You know I never do anything illegal. Hold on a sec, there's someone at the door."

I heard the phone rattle around some before Michael came back on the line. "Sorry about that. Just hooking up the encryption device. What's the plate number?"

I read him the number from the photograph. "Will you call me when you have the info?"

"You can hold if you're in a hurry."

"Jeez, is it that easy?"

"Only if you're gifted. Hang on."

He put the phone on speaker and I heard

rapid-fire keystrokes. Just for fun, I timed him. It took less than two minutes.

"Nina Jezek," he said. He spelled the last name and read me her home address and driver's license number.

"You're amazing."

"That's why they pay me the big bucks."

"Are you coming to the Bay Area any time soon? I'd like to buy you dinner."

"I might be in town next month. I have to present a security analysis to a board of directors in San Jose. Important people like to see your face when you give them bad news."

"Do you know the date?"

"Not yet. I'll call you."

"Thanks, Michael. You're the best."

I asked him to e-mail me a scan of Nina's driver's license. My e-mail pinged as I was hanging up the phone.

I enlarged the picture of her driver's license and sent it to the color printer. Then I e-mailed CIS, requesting a complete background report on Nina. I walked to the printer and picked up the page. Nina was thirty years old, five-eight and a hundred and twenty-seven pounds, with short brown hair and blue eyes. She didn't look like a killer. She looked intelligent, and pretty in a subdued way. Maybe Bill was right.

I printed four more copies, which I would distribute among my friends who were helping me shadow potential victims.

I needed to meet Nina and shake her hand. My intuition kicks in when I make physical contact with a subject. Plus I can tell a lot about someone by observing eye contact and body language, things you can't see in a photograph.

I typed and printed my notes from the conversation with Michael, (not mentioning his name), and tucked them, along with the photos of Nina, into Scott's file, which I locked in my Pendaflex drawer. I tried calling J.V. Trusty before leaving the office, but I got his voicemail.

Buddy and I drove back to the 1-Hour Photo and picked up my prints. I looked at them in the car. The pictures were clear, but they were profile shots and didn't show her eyes because of the sunglasses. I stuffed them in my purse before driving home. I didn't know if Bill would be dropping by tonight, and I didn't want him to see them. There was no point upsetting him until I knew something for sure.

〜

That night I surveyed a couple of restaurants and a bar, but I couldn't keep my mind on the job. I kept trying to think of a way to meet Nina.

Buddy and I got home a little after 10:00. I called Bill and asked when the next RCPD picnic was going to be.

"I never go to those," he said.

"I think we should go this year. I'd like to meet the other detectives."

"You just want to meet Nina. Leave it alone, Nikki. I told you, she's not the one."

"People are rarely who they appear to be."

After a moment of silence he said, "You're not going to let this go are you?"

"Nope."

"Fine. I'll see if I can arrange a tour of the department for you. I'll introduce you to all the detectives, the administrators, and the dispatchers, then I'll take you to records and introduce you to Nina. But you have to promise me that after you meet her you'll leave her alone."

"What if we hit it off and she wants to be friends?"

"Damn it Nikki!"

"Okay, okay. I promise." Of course he couldn't see that I had my fingers crossed.

CHAPTER 27

WHEN MY DREAM MACHINE WENT off
on Friday morning I hit the snooze
button and tried to go back to sleep, but
now Buddy was awake and needed a walk.
I dressed in sweats and started the coffee,
then walked him around the grounds. When
we got back to the boat I poured him some
kibble, and guzzled the coffee.

We drove to the gym and I got in a quick
workout, but managed to make it back to
the boat in time to call Bill before he left
for work.

"Can you set up the department tour for
this afternoon?" I asked hopefully.

"Maybe. Depends on what happens
today."

"Will you try?"

"I'll try," he sighed.

I showered and dressed, then Buddy and I walked up to the office. J.V. called my cell as I was unlocking the door.

"How did the physical go?" I asked.

"I'm fit as a fiddle."

"And the home study interview?"

"Passed with flying colors."

"Excellent. What's the next step?"

"Now they interview Scott to make sure he wants to live with me. If that goes well he moves in with me for a trial period. I can hardly wait!"

I was reminded once again of the positive aspects of this very disconcerting case.

We ended the call and I turned on the computer. I typed up my surveys from the previous night while I was waiting for Jim Sutherland and Jack McGuire to arrive. I had my reports and invoices completed by 10:00. Jim arrived at 10:02. Perfect timing.

Over coffee I told him about Nina Jezek and handed him an enlarged copy of her driver's license photo.

"She's pretty," he said. "Doesn't look like a killer, but you can't tell much from a picture."

"I might get a chance to meet her this afternoon," I said.

"Oh?"

"Bill's giving me a tour of the RCPD."

"What does he think about Nina?"

"He says there's no way."

"How well does he know her?"

"Not well. She works nights. He's only met her a couple of times."

"So, he could be wrong."

"It happens. I got this feeling when I took her picture yesterday. Like something was crawling up the back of my neck."

"Uh oh."

"Yeah. If I get the same feeling when I meet her, we'll need to shift our surveillance from the sex offenders to Nina."

"What hours does she work?"

"Four to midnight."

"I'll try free up some time for you, if it comes to that."

Jack joined us at 10:15. I gave him a copy of Nina's photo and filled him in on what I knew about her.

Jack would follow Vasey today, Jim would tail Morales, and I'd take Adamson. That way we were each shadowing someone who'd never seen us before. I gave them copies of the subject's files and told Jack that Vasey was driving a yellow and black pickup.

We walked out to the parking lot together. Jim followed me to Morales's address on Kramer Lane. I left him there and cruised around the corner to 5th, where Adamson lived. I pulled out his file and checked the photo. Gabriel Adamson was Caucasian, forty-six years old, five-ten, and a hundred and seventy pounds, with blond hair and blue eyes. He had a scruffy beard and mustache in the mug shot.

We were getting a late start today. I hoped Adamson wasn't already out stalking children. While I was waiting for some indication that he was home I glanced at Nina's photo again. I wanted to be sure I would recognize her if she jumped out of the bushes with a garlic-coated knife.

At 12:35 the drapes in Adamson's bungalow parted and I saw him for the first time. Dressed in a ratty pair of gray sweats and a wife-beater tee shirt, he scratched himself and yawned, then strolled away from the window. I got out my binoculars and tried to see inside the cottage, but the reflection from the sun on the window made it difficult.

I scanned the neighborhood while I waited for Adamson to come outside. I hoped Jim and Jack were having better luck.

At 1:10 I called Bill. He said we were on for the tour. He would meet me in the lobby at 3:45. Nina came to work at 4:00, but we would be going to the records department last. I hoped our visit wouldn't make her suspicious.

I felt a little rush of adrenaline. I can size most people up within five minutes and, given the opportunity to shake hands with the subject, I'm right ninety-nine percent of the time. Of course the one percent that I'm wrong almost got me killed last summer, but it's still only one percent.

At 1:35 I hooked Buddy to his leash and walked him around the neighborhood. He watered some trees and bushes, then had a drink from a bottle of water I'd brought along. I was just putting Buddy back in the car when Adamson's door opened. I pretended to be looking for my keys while watching him out of the corner of my eye. He locked the bungalow behind him and took off walking toward El Camino Real. I remembered Jack saying he'd taken the bus to Sequoia Station on Wednesday. I got in the car and waited to see which way he turned on El Camino. He went north. I drove to the corner and watched.

Adamson walked a block and a half and sat down at a bus stop. Tailing someone on a bus is a huge pain in the ass. You have to stay close to the bus, breathing the noxious exhaust fumes, and waiting for the subject to get off at every stop. I hoped he'd go to the Barnes & Noble again. That was only about six blocks and maybe three bus stops away.

Adamson boarded a northbound bus and I let a couple of cars get between us before following. No sense breathing any more fumes than I had to. When the bus stopped I pulled to the curb and watched passengers disembark. Adamson was still onboard. The bus made it through the light before the traffic had cleared enough for me to merge, so I got stuck. I grabbed my binoculars and watched two women get off at the next stop. The light turned green and I managed to catch up just before Sequoia Station.

I pulled to the curb in a no parking zone and hoped this would be Adamson's destination. Luck was with me. He got off the bus, and I pulled into the Sequoia Station parking lot. When I turned to see if he was headed for the Barnes & Noble, Adamson was nowhere in sight. I roared back out to the street just in time to see him make a right off El Camino onto James Avenue. The only thing down James was the Caltrain station. *Crap!* He was taking the train.

I made the right on James and passed Adamson, parked, and got out of the car.

I jogged to the platform and watched as he put money into a vending machine. He retrieved his purchase and sat down on a bench to wait. I hustled over to the vending machine. It was a ticketing machine. No way to tell where he was going. I could wait and see which direction the train went, but trying to follow someone on a train is ridiculous, unless you're on the train with them. I wasn't willing to leave Buddy alone in the car that long.

I waited until Adamson boarded the northbound train, noting that no one who looked like Nina Jezek had followed him.

Buddy and I drove back to the marina and took a long walk before going to The Diving Pelican for lunch. I ordered the Gorgonzola Salad and fed him half of the cheese and some of the lettuce. He also drank two glasses of ice water. By the time we were finished eating it was time for me to meet Bill.

Buddy and I pulled into the parking area in front of the police station at 3:42. I rolled down the windows enough for the breeze to blow through, cranked open the sunroof, and locked the car behind me, promising I'd be back pretty soon. Buddy gave me a look that never fails to make me feel guilty.

When I entered the lobby I spotted L Ketteridge behind the desk leading to administration. L is a petite and jovial blonde woman in her early fifties. We met the first time I had occasion to visit the Redwood City Police Department, which was also the day I met Bill. Apparently all administrative employees at the RCPD wear nametags with their first initial and last name, so I still only knew Ms. Ketteridge as L.

"Could you let Detective Anderson know I'm here?" I asked, handing her my business card.

"I know who you are, honey. How's everything going? You two getting along okay?"

Apparently L knew a great deal more about me than I knew about her.

"Great," I said. "He's giving me a tour of the station today."

"Well, it's about time. Everyone wants to meet the woman who finally got Bill Anderson to settle down."

I flushed with embarrassment, not knowing how to respond.

"I'll tell him you're here." She winked at me and picked up the phone, dialing an extension and murmuring something I couldn't hear into the receiver with a smirk on her angelic face.

A minute later Bill strode into the lobby. He smiled when he saw me, but the smile didn't reach his eyes and I knew why. I was pushing the boundaries of our budding relationship, treading into hallowed territory. Although Nina wasn't technically a cop, she was an employee of the RCPD and, therefore, family. For that reason alone I hoped I was wrong about her.

Bill took me through administration first, introducing me to an eccentric collection of employees including a woman with spiky black hair, gothic make-up, eyebrow and nose piercings, and attitude galore. L's first name turned out to be Lynette. She was the Records Supervisor, and when we reached her desk she showed me photos of her children and grandchildren, and of her cocker spaniels. I proudly shared a picture of Buddy that I carry in my wallet.

While we were in administration one of the detectives came in looking for some paperwork. Before Bill got the chance, Lynette said, "Mario, this is Nicoli Hunter, Bill's girlfriend."

I shook Mario's hand. He gave mine

a squeeze and looked me up and down appraisingly.

"Nice to meet you," I said, pulling my hand away and resisting the urge to wipe it on my jeans.

I'd been hoping to see Lieutenant Marcia Quinn. She had recently saved a childhood friend of mine from a crazed killer and I wanted to thank her again, but she wasn't in the office she shared with the Investigations Sergeant at the moment.

Bill ushered me through the atrium and into the detective bureau, also known as the 'back room'. I'd been in this area before, but hadn't actually met any of Bill's coworkers. The first detective he introduced me to was Diane Winslow, who was the only female in the room. She was about five-nine and around a hundred and sixty pounds, with brown hair pulled back at the nape of her neck, and brown eyes. She gave me her business card and said I should call any time I wanted to complain about Bill. Once again I had the feeling of intimacy, like there was already a relationship established between us. It made me feel welcome and uncomfortable at the same time.

There were two men in their thirties having a conversation by the window near

Bill's desk. He introduced me to Dale Gooden and Tom King. Both men were dressed in jeans, flannel shirts, thermal vests, and rubber soled hiking boots. Apart from being dressed alike, they interacted like siblings and they kind of looked alike. I wondered if working with a partner long term was like being married, and you started to resemble each other after a while. I shook Gooden and King's hands and they resumed their conversation.

Next Bill introduced me to the 911 dispatchers. There were four women and one man in a circular bullpen area. They were all casually dressed and extremely friendly. I had expected this area to be fraught with tension, but in fact it was the most relaxed department I'd been in so far. I shook everyone's hand and received yet another invitation, from a heavyset woman, to call her any time I needed to dish about Bill. I wondered what kind of complaints they expected me to have. Maybe they thought a civilian would need to talk about the stress of dating a cop. In fact, the opposite was more likely to be true. My job created more stress for Bill than his did for me.

Finally we arrived in records. I felt the goose flesh before we even passed through the doorway. Nina Jezek was seated in front of a flat panel monitor, entering data on an ergonomic keyboard. Her desk was devoid of any personal memorabilia. She probably shared it with a day shift employee.

She was dressed in jeans, Nikes, and a navy-blue polo shirt with the RCPD logo emblazoned on the chest. Her face was unlined and she looked about twenty-five, although I knew from her driver's license she was older. Her hair was light brown and cut short, framing an attractive face unadorned by make-up.

She looked up as we approached and I saw her lips curve into a smile when she made eye contact with Bill. Then her gaze shifted to me and the smile vanished. *Oh my God,* I thought, *she has a crush on him.*

Bill introduced us and I held out my hand. She hesitated, then slowly stood up and said, "Nice to meet you."

When she took my hand I felt the voltage shoot up my arm. Her grip was firm, her hand was cool and dry, and she was, without a doubt, the killer I had been seeking. I felt shock waves run through my psyche and fought the reflex to snatch my hand away.

"So this is the records department," I

said casually. "How long have you worked here, Nina?"

She released my hand and took a step back, moving behind her swivel chair.

"Almost two years," she said.

She and Bill made small talk for a few tense minutes, then we let Nina get back to work and reentered the atrium in the center of the building.

I sat down on a bench surrounding a large planter box and tried to breathe.

"You okay?" Bill asked.

"I have a headache. Do you have any aspirin?"

"Sure. Stay here, I'll be right back."

I glanced over my shoulder while he was gone, half expecting Nina to come at me from behind while I was alone. Of course that was silly. There was no way she could know I was working for the son of one of her victims. I was just spooked.

Bill came back a minute later with a bottle of Excedrin and a paper cup of water. I swallowed two of the pills and drank all the water.

"Thanks. Maybe I'll go home and lie down. I have to work tonight."

Bill walked me to my car and gave Buddy a head scratch, then stood there and watched me drive away. My gut twisted as I formulated a plan to catch Nina in the act. I hoped my relationship with Bill was strong enough to weather this.

Back at the office, I called Jack, Elizabeth, Jim, and Lily. Much to my relief they all agreed to meet with me at 6:00 that night.

CHAPTER 28

I BREWED A POT OF COFFEE, extra strong, lit a cigarette, and opened a blank Excel workbook on the computer. I created a timeline spreadsheet for the next seventy-two hours, starting at midnight tonight when Nina got off work. I'd take the first shift from midnight to 2:00 a.m., Jim would take 2:00 to 4:00 a.m., Elizabeth and Jack would share 4:00 to 8:00 a.m., and Lily would pick Nina up at 8:00. I'd relieve Lily at noon tomorrow.

I remembered J.V. was flying in tomorrow morning. I'd have to suggest a rental car so he could spend time with Scott while I was tailing Nina.

By 6:00 I was wired on caffeine and adrenaline. I waited until everyone was gathered in the office before outlining my plan. I went over the surveillance schedule and each of my friends accepted the shift I'd chosen for them, so I printed five copies of the spreadsheet and handed them out, giving Nina's driver's license photo, which Jim and Jack already had, to Lily and Elizabeth. No one questioned the fact that we were going to follow this woman around the clock based solely on my intuition.

I made sure everyone had each other's cell numbers before we parted company at 6:45.

Buddy and I took a walk around the marina, then went down to the boat and had dinner.

Bill called at 7:50.

"How's your headache?"

I felt a pang of guilt. "Better. I think I was just hungry. I'll be working late tonight. I have a couple of bar surveys to do in San Francisco and one of the owners wants me to stay until closing time."

This wasn't unusual. I often work until 2:00 a.m., but my tone of voice must have given me away because Bill was silent. I'm not a good liar and Bill has years of experience recognizing deceit.

"I'll be taking Buddy with me tonight," I added, hoping to divert his attention.

"Okay," he said.

"You want to get together tomorrow?"

"If I'm not working, sure." His tone was distant. He could tell I was hiding something.

After ending the call Buddy and I watched the news while cuddling on the pilothouse settee.

At 11:00 I dressed in black jeans and a black turtleneck, with my black leather jacket concealing the holster at the small of my back.

I got Buddy settled in the back seat of the Bimmer and drove to the RCPD, parking in a vacant lot across the street. At 12:04 Nina's black Celica rolled out through the security gate. She turned right on Maple and I followed at a distance. It's always easier to tail someone in the dark. Car headlights are less recognizable than the make, model, and color of a car.

We cruised up Woodside Road toward Highway 280. Nina made a left just past the Pioneer Saloon and then an immediate right into the Village Pub parking lot. I pulled into the lot behind her and parked a few rows away from the Celica.

I watched Nina climb out of her car wearing a voluminous white chiffon dress with ankle strap sandals. She had to be freezing. It wasn't more than fifty degrees outside.

The Village Pub is an elegant little restaurant that caters to the well-to-do residents of Woodside. I doubted they served dinner after 10:00 p.m., but the bar would be open.

I waited a minute before following Nina inside. As I entered I scanned the cocktail lounge to my right and spotted her seated at the end of the bar near a small group of well-dressed men who occupied a corner table. I chose a table as far from the exit as I could get and hoped Nina wouldn't spot me in the mirror behind the bar. I sat with my back to her, trying to be invisible.

The cocktail waitress approached my table and I ordered coffee. I glanced over my shoulder and saw the bartender serve Nina something pink in a tall glass with cherries and a straw. The men at the table on her left had taken notice of her, and no small wonder. Her dress was sheer and, although her curves were minimal, those she had were clearly displayed.

After a few minutes one of the men at the table rose and approached the bar. He stood near Nina while speaking with the bartender, and then turned to face her. He was a handsome dark-haired man in his late thirties. He smiled easily as he spoke, and I got a distinctly flirtatious vibe watching Nina's response. The bartender served the man his drink and he seated himself on the stool next to Nina's. She was concentrating on him now, and I was getting a stiff neck from watching over my shoulder, so I scooted my chair around for a better view.

The cocktail waitress served my coffee and asked if I wanted to run a tab.

"No thanks," I said, handing her a twenty. When she moved out of my line of sight I noted that the dark-haired guy was holding Nina's hand. Fast worker. I remembered Bill saying she was shy. Obviously he'd never seen her in a bar.

The guy was facing me and I could see Nina smiling demurely in the back bar mirror. I took a mental picture of the man, then looked up at the ceiling and spotted two surveillance cameras. One was directed at the cash register behind the bar, but the other was mounted above the mirror, facing the room. That one might get a clear shot of his face. Now all I had to do was figure out how to get a still shot from the video. If the Village Pub had an internal computer network there was a remote possibility the security cameras were run through it. If that was the case, Michael might be able to hack into the network and get me access to the footage. Of course, once I had his picture I still had to find out who he was. I thought about revisiting the sex offenders website searching for his face, and shuddered at the memory of what I'd read on those pages.

While I was mulling all this over in my head, Nina slipped off her barstool. I quickly turned my chair so my back was to her and took a compact out of my purse so I could watch what was happening without being seen. I pretended to put on lip gloss as I watched the man say something to his friends before escorting Nina outside.

Holy shit! Was she going home with this guy? I had to remind myself she was a cold-blooded killer and not the innocent she appeared to be. I collected my change from the table, leaving a tip, and moved toward the door.

When I reached the lot Nina's Celica was backing out of the parking space and a shiny new Mercedes Roadster was idling near the exit. I turned my head so my hair covered my face and hurried to the BMW.

Buddy and I got to Woodside Road in time to see the Celica following the roadster toward Highway 280. I made the left turn and gave chase. They stayed on Woodside Road until it became La Honda Road, and then made a right onto Skywood Way, and another right on Ranch Road. The roadster pulled into a driveway and Nina parked on the street. I quickly shut off my headlights and stopped at the intersection of Skywood and Ranch.

My whole body was thrumming with anticipation. A sex offender who could afford to live in the Woodside Hills might have bought his way out of trouble. I checked the luminous dial on my watch. It was 1:47 a.m. I desperately wanted a cigarette, but smoke is visible even at night, and I needed to remain in the shadows.

Nina got out of her car and sashayed up the driveway. I took out my cell phone and called Jim. I couldn't see the address but I gave him directions and described the house, which was a two-story Georgian-style brick. It wouldn't be hard for him to spot my car. The houses in this neighborhood were at least an acre apart, and Nina's Celica and my BMW were the only cars parked on the street.

Once Nina was inside I took out my camera and shot a couple pictures of the front of the house. Then I rolled down my window, lit a cigarette, and waited for Jim.

CHAPTER 29

N INA HAD FOLLOWED GIORDANO TO *the Village Pub the previous Saturday night and decided to take the chance that he might show up there again. Because Giordano favored slender young women she had chosen a dress that accentuated her lack of assets. The taser was in her purse, in case he didn't approach her. If that happened her plan was to follow him home and stun him when he got out of his car. Last week he had parked in his driveway, so she assumed he'd do the same thing tonight.*

Nina had been unnerved by Anderson's visit with his PI girlfriend. There was something disturbing about Nicoli Hunter. When they shook hands she'd had the feeling Hunter could almost read her mind.

She had changed clothes and put on make-up during her dinner break. Being the only swing shift employee in the records department had its benefits. After work she'd driven to the Village Pub and immediately spotted Giordano's Mercedes. She parked nearby, checked her image in the rearview mirror, and took a deep breath. This would be the first time she had attempted to seduce a target before taking him out. She wasn't sure she had the skills required. Nina had never been good with men. The ones who were attracted to her always wanted to be in control, and Nina could not allow herself to be dominated.

She'd entered the restaurant and gone directly to the bar, ordering a Shirley Temple with an extra cherry and a straw. Giordano was at the same table he and his friends had occupied the previous weekend. Sipping her drink, she'd glanced in his direction, made eye contact and smiled, then quickly looked away. The second time she glanced at him he'd said something to his friends, gotten up, and come over to the bar. He'd ordered a Kettle One martini on the rocks, then turned to her and said, "How you doin' tonight?" His speech was imprecise, making him sound like he had a cold. Nina knew it was because of the missing tip of his tongue.

"I'm fine," she'd said. "Maybe a little bored with the nightlife in this town."

"Really? You don't look like the kind of girl who craves excitement."

"I might surprise you," she'd said.

When Giordano's drink was served he'd swallowed half of it and seated himself next to her.

"What's your name sweetheart?"

"Nina. What's yours?"

"Alfredo Giordano. You can call me Fredo."

"Nice to meet you, Fredo."

"It's very nice to meet you, Nina." He'd put his hand on top of hers. "Can I buy you a drink?"

"Actually, I don't need another drink. I was here last weekend and I saw you with your friends. I came back tonight thinking I might get to meet you."

She hoped his ego was inflated enough to buy her act.

Giordano had scrutinized her for a moment. "Is that right?" he'd said. "Well, why don't we go to my place and get to know each other."

"I'd like that," Nina said, with a coy smile.

"I'll tell my friends we're leaving."

As they'd walked outside Nina had taken his arm and leaned into him. "Do you mind if I follow you? I'll feel more secure if I have my own car in the morning."

"Whatever you want, sweetheart."

She'd followed him up into Woodside Hills and made a point of parking on the street when they reached his house. She didn't want her car to be seen in his driveway. He probably had security cameras on the property. She hoped he didn't have any in the bedroom.

Giordano parked his Benz and waited for Nina to join him before unlocking the front door. He ushered her into the foyer and she watched as he keyed in his security code. Nina's memory wasn't photographic, but it was very good.

"Would you like a drink?" Giordano asked.

Nina wanted Giordano as intoxicated as possible. He was a big man and she would need him to be relaxed for what she had in mind.

"I'll have whatever you're having," she said.

Giordano escorted Nina into the living room where he had a beautifully appointed wet bar. He was having another Kettle One martini. He mixed their drinks in an old fashioned cocktail shaker and poured them into rocks glasses.

Nina scanned the ceiling for cameras, but didn't see anything obvious. She took a sip of the drink and smiled. It was very strong.

Giordano ran his fingers up her arm. "I like your dress," he said.

"I bought it for you."

"I'm flattered."

"You're a very attractive man. You must be used to women throwing themselves at you."

"It happens."

"This is an amazing house," Nina said. "May I have a tour?"

"Absolutely."

She set her drink on the bar and picked up her purse. Giordano took her hand and led her into the foyer. Her heart raced as they climbed the stairs. He drew her into the master bedroom, downed the last of his drink, and kissed her fingertips.

"This is the playroom," he said, pulling her close and thrusting his stubby tongue into her mouth.

Nina allowed the kiss and then leaned away, placing a hand on his chest.

"There are a couple of things you should know about me," she said. "I need to be on top." Giordano smiled. "And I'm into bondage." His eyebrows rose as she opened her purse and took out four lengths of soft rope. "I hope you're not afraid of being restrained."

CHAPTER 30

J IM PULLED UP BEHIND ME at 2:11 a.m. He got out of his car and joined me in mine.

"What's happening?"

I pointed out the house and Nina's Celica. "She's inside with a guy she met at the Village Pub. I have no idea who he is, but I'd be willing to bet he's going to regret meeting her."

"Should we call the cops?"

"And tell them what? We have no evidence that she's the killer. Besides, he may not be a victim. Maybe she just wants to get laid."

"So, now what?"

"I'd like to stay here until she comes out, but there's no telling how long she'll be in there. Keep an eye on the front door. If she hasn't come out by 3:30, call Jack and

Elizabeth and give them directions. If she comes out with blood on her dress call the cops and then call me. I won't be able to sleep anyway." I reached out and touched his arm. "Thank you for doing this, Jim."

"No problem," he said, giving my hand a pat, then went back to his own car.

I pulled into the marina parking lot at 2:40, shut off the engine and sat in the car, thinking. I considered unlocking the office and sending a quick e-mail to Michael, asking if he could try to hack into the Village Pub's computer network and access their security monitors. Of course, if Nina's date for the night survived there would be no reason to ID him. If he didn't, I'd know soon enough who he was. It would be all over the news.

I got out of the car and walked Buddy around on the lawn while he did his business. Then we trudged down to the boat.

I took off my clothes, climbed into bed, and closed my eyes for a minute. When I opened them again the sun was shining through the portlight curtains. I checked the bedside clock. It was after 8:00. I dove for my purse and checked my cell. I had two new voicemail messages. The first message had come in at 4:06 a.m., and was from Jim.

"She just came out of the house and her dress looks clean. Jack and Elizabeth are going to take it from here. Call me back after noon."

No blood on her dress. Could I have been wrong about Nina?

The second message was from Elizabeth and had been left at 4:51 a.m. "Hi, honey. We followed her to a sweet little cottage on Douglas Avenue in Burlingame. She has climbing roses. Do killers garden?"

I took a long, hot shower and then started coffee, scooped kibble into Buddy's dish, and ate some yogurt while the coffee dripped into the pot. After two cups I felt slightly more alert. I got dressed and took Buddy for a walk. After disposing of his morning offering I unlocked the office and checked my e-mail. I had one from CIS with the background on Nina. I printed it out and stuffed it in my purse. I had to meet J.V. at the airport.

I made it to SFO before his flight arrived and, after we met up at baggage claim, I explained what was happening and walked him to the Hertz desk. J.V. wanted to spend the day with Scott, but he was up for a night shift watching Nina. I suggested he rent a Camry or a Civic, in order to be inconspicuous.

"I *have* done this before, Nicoli," he said, with a gentle smile.

"Sorry. I keep forgetting you're a PI."

I followed J.V. to the Brewster's house and collected the prepaid cell and charger from Scott after J.V. presented him with his new iPhone. Scott seemed happy to see his uncle and was delighted with his new cell phone. He gave Buddy a long hug before we left, and was openly disappointed that we weren't going to be spending the day with him, or at least that Buddy wasn't. I reminded myself how much I was doing for this kid, and tried to get over the fact that he missed my dog. Besides, soon he would have his own dog to love.

Buddy and I set off to meet Lily in Burlingame where she was watching Nina's cottage. My shift didn't start until 12:00, so I'd be early, but I didn't have anything more important to do and I was sure Lily would be happy to be relieved.

I drove to Douglas Avenue and spotted Lily's van. I parked behind her and called her on my cell.

"Any activity?" I asked.

"Nope. She's probably asleep. I hear she had a late night."

"She didn't get home until almost five. You can leave if you want."

"Okay. Have fun."

I hunkered down for what I guessed would be a very boring couple of hours. As Lily drove away I began to think about what I would do if Nina didn't attempt to kill anyone in the next few days. I could probably recruit Jack to let me into her house while she was at work, so I could search for evidence. I can pick a lock, but Jack is much faster and in a residential neighborhood speed counts. If I found proof that Nina was the killer I wouldn't be able to take it to the police, but at least I'd know I was on the right track.

After watching the house for almost an hour my sleep-deprived brain remembered that she knew what I looked like. I pulled a baseball cap out of my glove box and stuffed my hair up underneath it, put on my sunglasses, and slumped down in the seat.

Another thirty minutes passed before I remembered I had the background report from CIS in my purse. I dug it out and began reading.

Nina Jezek had been born at San Francisco General Hospital. Her mother's maiden name was Anezka Kamila Sedlak,

and her father was Kazimir Miklos Jezek.
They were both Czechoslovakian. Kazimir
and Anezka had immigrated before Nina was
born, and she had grown up in Pacifica, on
the California coast, attending grade school
and high school there.

She'd received a scholarship and had
earned a bachelor's degree in communications
from Georgetown University in Washington
D.C. During college she'd worked at a
Round Table Pizza. After graduation she had
accepted a position as a junior editor with
Georgetown Magazine, and had worked there
until she was twenty-seven. She had been
in the Bay Area for a visit on her birthday
when her father had committed suicide.

I flipped to the page that showed her
financial history. Nina's father had named
her as the sole beneficiary of a substantial
life insurance policy. After his death she had
moved back from D.C. She had initially
rented the cottage on Douglas Avenue, but
six months after signing the lease she had
purchased the property.

I set the report aside and tried to picture
Nina's life. She'd done well enough in school
to receive a scholarship to Georgetown, and
upon graduation had been offered what I
was sure was a coveted position on campus.

Then three years ago her father had taken his own life while she was in town, and on her birthday. Then she'd moved back to California. Why? To be near her mother? I glanced at the report. Anezka Jezek was still living in the house where Nina had grown up. She would be in her late fifties. Maybe they were close. What was hard to understand was Nina taking her degree in communications and going to work as a swing shift data entry clerk at the Redwood City Police Department. Why not find a position where she could make use of her degree and earn a decent salary? The only reason I could think of was that she wanted access to the databases.

Her priorities had changed when her father killed himself. If he had molested her as a child she might not have felt safe living near him. Also, if she was an abused child she might be acting out a lifelong fantasy of getting even, except that her father was dead, so she would need to find someone else to punish. I wondered if she had actually killed her own father and made it look like a suicide.

I finished reading the financial report. Six months ago all of Nina's savings had been transferred to a numbered Swiss account.

I glanced up at the cottage. The drapes had been opened, but Nina was nowhere in sight. Her Celica was still parked in the driveway.

I read the rest of the background, but there was nothing more interesting than a parking ticket she had received in Sunnyvale last month. That stirred something in my memory, but it was fuzzy. I needed a nap.

At 1:45 I called Jim and told him where I was. His Volvo rolled up the street at 2:14. I called his cell.

"She's awake," I said, "but no activity so far this afternoon. You get any sleep?"

"Some. How are you doing?"

"I've been better. Thanks again for doing this, Jim. You're a prince."

"Yes, I am."

CHAPTER 31

C∼⊙ ⊙∽

NINA HAD NO PROBLEM GETTING *Giordano out of his clothes and onto the bed, and only a little trouble fending off his attempts to undress her before she tied his wrists and ankles to the bedposts. When she was certain he was secure, she'd slipped off her dress, shoes, and undergarments, and placed them on a chair. Watching her, Giordano had quickly developed an erection. Then Nina took a pair of latex gloves out of her purse and watched Giordano's hard-on soften.*

"What are you doing?" he'd asked.

"I have some questions, Fredo."

She'd removed the switchblade from her bag and Giordano had begun thrashing around on the bed, trying to loosen the knots.

"Every time you don't answer honestly, I'm going to cut you. This knife is coated with

*garlic. Garlic is an anticoagulant, so wherever
I cut you the blood won't clot. You'll just keep
bleeding. Is that clear?"*

*"What the fuck do you want, you crazy
bitch?"*

*"I want your client and supplier lists. I
want to know about all the perverts you sell
children to, and the ones you buy them from.
If you give me the lists I might let you live."*

"You can go to hell."

"You first," Nina said, and sliced his thigh.

*Giordano squealed, lifting his head to see
the blood oozing from the wound.*

*"You see how that's bleeding? If I cut a
little higher I might accidentally nick an
artery. Where are the lists?"*

*Less than an hour later Nina had Gior-
dano's client list and a list of men and women
in other countries from whom he purchased
children for his customers. She saved them on a
CD and erased the files from his computer. She
tried not to think about what happened to the
children when Giordano's clients tired of them.*

*He'd told her where his security room
was, and she had removed the surveillance
video discs and disabled all of the cameras.
There would be no record that she had ever
been there.*

When she had everything she'd come

*for, Nina stabbed Giordano in the heart
and watched him die. Then she showered in
his bathroom, carefully cleaning the drain
afterwards. She dressed, donned a fresh pair
of latex gloves, and went downstairs to the
laundry room. Placing the towel she had used
in the washer, she added bleach and turned
it on. When the laundry was in the dryer
she collected her belongings, entered the code
to turn off the alarm, and was out the door
shortly after 4:00 a.m.*

CHAPTER 32

B UDDY AND I ARRIVED BACK at the
marina a little before 3:00 on Saturday
afternoon. I opened the office and dropped
Nina's background report on my desk,
checked my e-mail and voicemail, and then
walked down to the boat, determined to get
some sleep.

Bill had left me a voicemail message
saying he was at the office, but would be
free for dinner. J.V. had called asking what
time his Nina shift would be tonight. I
called J.V. first and told him I'd meet him at
Bill's house at 9:30. Then I called Bill and
said that dinner sounded great, but I'd have
to make it an early night.

"Are you working again tonight?" he
asked.

"I have to. Sorry. Till-tapping bartender.

I thought I might need a second pair of eyes, so J.V. is coming along."

I caught what might have been a sigh, or maybe it was just my overactive conscience.

"We haven't had much time together lately, have we," I said.

"It's okay. Do you want to go out for dinner, or should I get take-out?"

"I have to hit the road at 8:30, so take-out makes more sense."

"Any preference?"

"Whatever you want."

"I like the sound of that."

Bill arrived at 6:45 and we shared the Crouching Tiger's spicy Sichuan & Hunan take-out with Buddy. I was feeling tense and guilty, but tried to make up for it by seducing Bill before I left to meet J.V. After that he was happy to stay on the boat with Buddy while I went out.

I stopped at the office and went over the Nina-watch schedule. J.V. and I would work together tonight, but tomorrow he would take a shift by himself. I extended the schedule through Wednesday afternoon. If we didn't have anything on Nina by then, I'd ask Jack to let me into her house while she was at work.

After inserting J.V. into the schedule I

sent it as an e-mail attachment to Elizabeth,
Jack, Lily, and Jim. I called Jim, waking him
up, and he told me that Nina had spent an
hour and a half at the RCPD that afternoon.
That was weird. It was Saturday.

Elizabeth and Jack had watched Nina
until 8:00, when Lily took over, so I called
them and suggested they check their e-mail.

I printed a copy of the schedule for
myself and one for J.V.

J.V. was waiting outside Bill's house
when I pulled to the curb, and a non-descript
Camry was parked in the driveway. I got out
of the car and gave him a hug.

"How did it go with Scott today?"

"Great! We went to the San Francisco
Zoo. You ever been there?"

"Many times. Which animals did Scott
like the best?"

"Monkey island."

"I love Monkey Island. Did you see
Bill today?"

"Nope. House was empty when I got
here. Why?"

"I forgot to tell you the subject we're
watching is an RCPD employee. Bill doesn't
know about the surveillance."

"Do you think that's a good idea, him
not knowing?"

"For the moment, yes. If my suspicions

about her are confirmed I'll have to tell him, of course."

I called Lily's cell and J.V. stood by waiting to hear the plan for tonight.

"Hi, Nikki."

"Hi, sweetie. What's Nina up to?"

"She left the house a few minutes after eight, drove to San Francisco, and parked on Twenty-Fourth Street in Noe Valley. Sat in her car for forty-five minutes, and then drove to a neighborhood grocery. Before she got out of her car she put on a red knit cap and a pair of horn rimmed glasses. She's inside the store now. I didn't think she could get in too much trouble in a grocery store, so I'm waiting in the parking lot."

"Call me when she comes out," I said.

"Will do."

I turned to J.V. and said, "We have a little time to kill. Lily says Nina is at a grocery in San Francisco."

I followed him into the house and we sat in the living room, going over the schedule. I had him down from 8:00 to 10:00 tomorrow night.

"When are you flying home?" I asked.

"Monday morning. Eight to ten tomorrow is fine."

Lily called at 9:40. She was on the road

again, driving south on Highway 101. She promised to call as soon as Nina stopped somewhere, and mentioned that she had heard sirens as they were pulling out of the grocery store parking lot.

"Fire engine, EMS, or police sirens?"

"Only you would ask a question like that. How the fuck should I know what kind of sirens they were?"

"It was probably nothing."

She called again at 9:55 to say that Nina was home and had closed the curtains after entering the house. Excellent.

J.V. and I hopped in the Camry and drove to Burlingame. I called Lily as we pulled up behind her van.

"No activity," she said.

"Thanks, Lily. Have a good night."

J.V. and I sat across the street and half a block down from Nina's cottage until 1:30 a.m. Then I called Jim and told him where we were.

I saw the midnight blue Volvo approaching at 1:55, so when my phone rang I assumed it was Jim and didn't check the display.

"Right on time," I said.

"Nikki, it's Lily. I'm watching the news. You know that grocery store in Noe Valley that Nina went into?"

"Yeah." I felt an icy sense of dread twist through my stomach.

"A guy was killed there tonight. Stabbed, at approximately 9:35."

The silence stretched between us, then my phone made a clicking sound and I knew Jim was trying to call me. "Hang on a sec, Lily." I switched to the incoming call.

"Jim?"

"Yeah."

"Can I call you right back?"

"Sure."

I reconnected with Lily. "Did you get his name?"

"Oscar Rossi. Forty-two years old. And get this, they showed a picture of his home on TV. It's right across the street from where Nina was parked before she drove to the store. I thought you'd want to know."

I scribbled some hasty notes. "Thanks, Lily. Get some sleep. You'll have to make a statement to the police tomorrow. You can tell them you saw a woman running out of the store and heard sirens. Give them her description and license plate number."

"I don't have her license plate number."

It was too dark for me to read the plate on the Celica. "I've got it at the office," I said. "I'll call you with it in the morning."

"All right. But I don't know how I'm going to explain what I was doing at a market in Noe Valley when I live in Redwood City."

"It probably won't come up, but if it does just say you were having drinks at a bar and decided to do some shopping before going home."

"What if they ask to see my receipt?"

"I doubt they'll ask for your receipt."

"What if the store has security cameras, and they watch the tape, and I'm not on it?"

"You could say that when you were getting out of your car you realized you didn't have your wallet. Nina came running out of the store and you heard sirens, so you jotted down her license plate number. Then you drove back to the bar and found your wallet in the parking lot."

"That's good. What's the name of the bar?"

"I'll tell you that when I give you Nina's plate number in the morning."

"Okay."

"Sweet dreams."

"Yeah, like I'm going to sleep after this."

I called Jim back and told him about Oscar Rossi.

"*Jesus*," he said.

"Don't let your guard down, and keep your car doors locked."

"Will do."

"Are you armed?"

"Of course."

"Okay. I'll talk to you tomorrow."

J.V. and I drove back to Redwood City in silence. He pulled into Bill's driveway and parked, then turned to face me.

"You need to tell Bill what's happening."

"I know, and I will, just not yet."

"Secrets aren't good for a relationship."

"I don't normally keep secrets from Bill, but he made me promise I wouldn't bother Nina."

"You're not bothering her. You're shadowing her. There's a difference."

"I don't think he'll see it that way."

"Maybe you're not giving him enough credit."

"It's this whole brotherhood thing," I said. "He's normally a very rational person, but when it comes to his fellow officers he has a blind spot."

"Nina's a data entry clerk."

"Doesn't matter. She works for the police department, so she's family."

"Do what you think is best, but if she kills again and you could have prevented it by telling Bill, you're going to hate yourself."

Chapter 33

N INA HAD LOGGED INTO THE *DMV*
database on Saturday afternoon. She'd
enlarged and printed the driver's license
photos of the eleven pedophiles on Giordano's
client list.

She'd popped the CD she had made at
Giordano's house into her computer and
read about each man's proclivities and the
frequency of his transactions. After reading
all the sordid details she'd selected Oscar Rossi
as her next target. Rossi made an average
of four purchases a year from Giordano. He
preferred developmentally challenged Hispanic
boys between the ages of six and nine. Nina
couldn't wait to end his life.

She'd driven to Rossi's neighborhood in
San Francisco that night, hoping he would
come outside. Since he wasn't a man she could

entice to a secluded location, she would have to take him in public. It wouldn't be the first time, but it increased the risk. She had brought along a red knit cap her grandmother had crocheted for her, and a pair of horn-rimmed glasses that she'd purchased at the drugstore. The color of the hat was so bold that it would distract anyone from looking at her face, plus it covered her hair. The glasses would obscure her features. Other than that she would have to rely on her ability to blend into her surroundings.

CHAPTER 34

◯ ◯ ◯

I PULLED INTO THE MARINA PARKING lot at 2:40 a.m., locked the car, and shuffled to the gate feeling drained. As I was inserting my magnetic key in the lock I heard canine toenails clicking up the metal companionway. I opened the gate and caught eighty-five pounds of wiggling puppy in my arms.

"Did you come all the way up here alone?" I asked, squatting down to nuzzle Buddy's silky ears. When I stood to walk down the ramp I saw Bill approaching on the dock, wearing nothing but a pair of jeans.

"I told him to stay," he grumbled. "He needs obedience training."

"Good idea."

Like I had time to take him to class. I didn't think it would make a difference anyway. I had a feeling Buddy would do whatever suited him, regardless. We walked back to the boat with Buddy prancing along beside us, happy that his pack was together again.

I undressed, leaving my clothes on the floor, set the alarm for 9:00, and crawled into bed. Bill wrapped himself around me and kissed me on the neck, quadrupling the guilt I was already feeling.

I slept fitfully, my subconscious trying to find a way to apprehend Nina without telling Bill what I was doing. When the alarm went off I hit the snooze button and tried to go back to sleep, but my attention was caught by an aroma that made my mouth water. Bacon. I struggled into a sitting position, inhaled deeply, and climbed out of bed.

Bill and Buddy were in the galley reading the Sunday paper and eating kibble. I wondered if Rossi's murder had made the headlines.

There was an empty plate on the counter in front of Bill.

"Tell me you saved me some bacon," I whimpered.

"On the stove."

I snatched a plate from the cabinet and greedily scooped up the remaining two strips. There was another pan with scrambled eggs in it. I emptied that onto my plate as well. I filled a mug with coffee and plunked everything down on the galley counter.

After breakfast and a walk, I took Buddy with me to the office and looked up Nina's license plate number in Scott's file. I did a Google search for bars in Noe Valley, selecting one near 24th Street and, for good measure, I looked up the number of the San Francisco Police Department serving Noe Valley. Then I called Lily and gave her all the info.

"Call the cops from your cell," I suggested. "What's Nina up to this morning?"

"She's still in the house."

I logged onto the Meagan's Law website and looked for Oscar Rossi, but he wasn't registered. I Googled him and read the report of his death online. There was no mention of a suspect in the case.

I walked Buddy around the marina and then back down to the boat, leaving him with Bill. I changed into my sweats and drove to the gym where I added an extra thirty minutes of StairMaster to my workout, in penance for the bacon. Then I took a sauna before showering to work some of the kinks out of my neck and shoulders.

I was back at the office by 11:30. I called
Lily again.

"Any activity?" I asked.

"She's parked on Winchester Drive
in Atherton. Listen, I've been wearing a
different wig every time I follow her, but I'm
going to need to change cars if this goes on
much longer."

"How long has she been on Winchester?"

"About twenty minutes."

"I'm on my way. Call my cell if she
moves."

I thought about what Lily had said. Even
though there were five of us taking shifts,
our cars would begin to register with Nina
before long. If she didn't get arrested soon
I'd have to spring for five rental cars.

I locked up the office and called Bill as I
walked to the parking lot.

"Emergency lunch survey," I said. "Be
back around two-thirty."

"Bring us a doggy bag."

"Sure." *Crap*. Now I'd actually have to
go to a restaurant.

I donned my baseball cap and sunglasses
and set out for Atherton. I found Winchester
Drive easily enough and spotted Nina's
Celica parked on the corner. I pulled to the

curb a block away from Lily's van and called her cell.

"I'm here," I said. "What's up?"

"About five minutes ago she got out of her car carrying a clipboard, and walked down the driveway of that pink stucco monstrosity on the corner. She's wearing a navy-blue jumpsuit with some kind of a patch on the left breast."

"Can you see down the driveway from where you're sitting?"

"No. I lost sight of her about twenty yards down the drive."

Since we didn't have any evidence a crime was being committed, there was no point calling the cops.

"What about a house number?" I asked.

"Hang on."

I saw Lily get out of her van and jog to the corner. She checked the mailbox in front of the estate, then jogged back to her van and told me the address.

"Go home," I said. "I'll take it from here."

We disconnected and I called Michael Burke. Amazingly, he answered after only two rings.

"Hello, Nikki."

"You're answering your phone now?"

"I'm keeping it plugged into the encryption device."

"I need a big favor in a big hurry."

"What else is new?"

I gave him the address on Winchester and said I needed all the information he could get on the owner. I held while he put the phone on speaker, and listened to his fingers hammer the keyboard.

"Owner's name is Anthony Costa. Age thirty-eight, Caucasian, five-eleven and one-eighty-five, according to his driver's license. Brown hair and eyes. Hang on." There were more keystrokes, and then, "He's single. Never been married. Made his money in textiles, or rather his father did. Anthony has a very healthy stock portfolio."

He gave me a few additional details about Costa's family, how many sisters and brothers he had, where his father was buried, things like that.

"Will you e-mail me all the data?"

"Sure."

"Thanks, Michael. You could do this for a living."

"Very funny."

What Michael had told me about Costa only confirmed that he had enough money to live in this neighborhood. Nina's presence here suggested that he was single because he preferred having sex with children.

I was still trying to make up my mind whether I should risk approaching the house when I spotted Nina. She was moving quickly, dressed as Lily had described and still carrying the clipboard. The patch on her left breast was an RCPD emblem. I'd never seen any Redwood City police wearing jumpsuits, but she could have sewn the patch on herself.

She jumped into the Celica, started it up, and made a U-turn. I ducked below the dashboard as she roared past my car. Then I heard a high-pitched mewing sound, like a cat fight. I didn't want to think about what else the sound might be. I gave chase, catching up with Nina as she turned south on El Camino Real.

I kept my distance as she drove down Valparaiso to Middlefield and made a left, then took a right on Marsh Road. She was headed for the freeway. We merged into traffic on Highway 101 going north. Nina didn't exceed the speed limit and traffic was moderate, so it was easy for me to stay with her. As we approached Burlingame she flipped on her turn signal, changed lanes, and took the Broadway exit.

Now that I knew she was going home I could afford to keep my distance. Instead of following her directly, I took a different route, arriving from the opposite direction. When I made the turn onto Douglas the Celica was parked in the driveway and Nina was getting out of the car. I parked at the end of the street behind an SUV, wanting the additional cover.

Nina didn't leave her house again during my shift. I called Jim at 1:45 and told him about her activities earlier in the day, and where I was. He parked at the opposite end of the street at 2:05, and I took off.

I stopped at Cafe Figaro on Broadway and picked up an order of Linguine alla Mediterranea, which is linguine with tiger prawns, garlic, olive oil, olives, mushrooms, green onions, feta cheese, and white wine, for Bill and Buddy.

Driving home, I considered the situation I'd gotten myself into. Bill and I had been dating for five months now. He was spending most of his weekends with me on the boat, and I was becoming attached. I knew at some point he would find out I'd been following Nina. I was just putting off the inevitable, unless she somehow got caught without my involvement. That could happen.

Back at the marina I stopped in at the office and ate half of the pasta, so it would look like leftovers. I checked my e-mail and printed the one from Michael, which included a photo of Anthony Costa.

While the file was printing I considered Nina's recent activities. Something had changed. The guys she was going after now weren't registered sex offenders. I knew Rossi wasn't registered, and Michael would have said something if Costa had been. So what did these guys have in common? Costa and Rossi were both Italian. I remembered the man Nina had gone home with on Friday night. He'd looked Italian too. Had she changed her mind about killing off child molesters and decided, instead, to go after the Mafia? I know, not all Italians are associated with organized crime, but what other possible connection could there be?

I tucked the information about Costa into Scott's file, locked it back in the Pendaflex drawer, and walked down to the boat.

Buddy was waiting for me on deck, his leash tied to the pilothouse door. I unhooked it from his collar and followed him inside.

"Hello?"

"Hey, babe. I thought you might stop at the office before coming down, so I decided to restrain the dog so he couldn't take off on his own again."

"Good thinking. Want some pasta?"

"What kind?"

"Seafood."

"Excellent."

Bill and Buddy shared the contents of the to-go box while I popped the top off a bottle of Guinness and sat down at the galley counter. I sat there watching them eat, savoring the intimacy.

We spent the afternoon together, walking Buddy around the wildlife refuge and then reading on deck. Later I made a run to the grocery store and picked up some fresh salmon and lemon pepper marinade. Bill barbecued the fish while I tossed a green salad, and we ate outside, watching the sunset.

After dinner I said I needed to type up my lunch survey and hustled up to the office. I called Jim, who said Nina had not ventured out during his watch. Elizabeth and Jack were on duty now, so I called her cell.

"She's still at home, honey."

This was good news. I didn't know what she might have done to Costa this morning, but at least she was taking a break.

I called J.V. Trusty and told him my

cell phone would be turned off because I would be with Bill, but he could leave me a voicemail message if anything happened while he was watching Nina.

"Still haven't told him, eh?"

"Not yet. I'm hoping I won't have to."

"I don't want to tell you how to live your life, Nicoli, but if I were you I'd come clean. If he finds out on his own it'll be much worse."

"I know. I'll think about it."

I locked up the office and moseyed back down to the boat. I was scheduled to relieve J.V. at 10:00 and I hadn't told Bill I was going out again tonight. The lies were mounting up.

When I stepped aboard I said, "Bad news."

"Don't tell me."

"I have to do a bar survey tonight."

"You never sleep."

"I should print that on my business cards."

"Want me to go with you?"

"Thanks, but you have to work tomorrow. I'd feel guilty."

"Where are you going?"

"Tied House in Mountain View."

"What time do you have to be there?"

"At ten."

"You have time for a nap."

"That's not a bad idea."

I shucked off my clothes and got into bed, setting the Dream Machine for 9:00. I opened my paperback and tried to read myself to sleep, but my subconscious wasn't having any. I gave up at 8:30, climbing out of bed and into the shower.

CHAPTER 35

⸎

NINA ENJOYED CHECKING COSTA OFF her list. He hadn't been easy. He lived in Atherton, a town noted for its high crime rate, so the Redwood City Police Department logo on her jumpsuit had only made him suspicious, and she'd had to use the taser. He'd shuddered a few times, then dropped like a bag of rocks. She had dragged him into the foyer and quickly finished him off with the knife. As she rose to leave, she'd heard a woman's voice coming from the back of the house. "Who is it, Tony?"

Nina had bolted out the door, quickly closing it behind her, and had barely made it to the street before the screaming started.

There were nine men left on her list of Giordano's clients. If she managed to kill all of them, she'd think about going after the monsters from whom he had purchased the children. She'd need a fake passport and ID if she was going to do that. Nina didn't know anyone who could supply her with the documents, but she knew they were out there. She could probably use the RCPD database to locate an expert forger who had recently been paroled.

Next on her list of deviants was Marc Jensen. Jensen liked little girls. He'd made a purchase every six months for the last two years. He was a forty-four year old stockbroker living on Buena Vista Drive in Los Altos Hills. Since the near disaster with Costa, Nina had the feeling she was running out of time. She considered buying a gun, but there was a two-week waiting period in California. The taser would have to do.

CHAPTER 36

I DRESSED IN JEANS AND A turtleneck, sliding the Galco holster onto my belt. I checked my purse, making sure I still had the Ruger, kissed Bill goodbye, and told Buddy I'd be back pretty soon. His ears went flat against his head and his tail drooped. Bill told me to *be safe* as I went out the door.

I trudged up to my car feeling cranky and guilt-ridden. I knew it was only a matter of time before Bill heard about the Rossi killing, and I had no doubt there would be garlic in the wound.

It crossed my mind how ironic it was that Nina's break from her original pattern of killing child molesters was what had gotten me involved. When she killed Scott's mom she had set in motion the investigation that would probably lead to her arrest.

I wondered how Nina would react to having a pair of homicide detectives show up on her doorstep. They would know she worked for the RCPD. Would that alter the investigation? Would they contact the Internal Affairs department before questioning her? I was giving myself a headache, so I tried to stop thinking.

I started the car before calling J.V.'s cell number.

"Hiya boss," he said.

"Hey, J.V. Any movement tonight?"

"I'm in Los Altos on Buena Vista. Ms. Jezek is parked at the end of the street, sitting in her car. Been here about five minutes."

"Okay. What's she wearing?"

"Red cocktail dress, high heels, small shoulder bag, blonde wig."

"She's wearing a wig?"

"Yep."

"That can't be good. I'm on my way. Call me if she gets out of her car."

I didn't know Los Altos well enough to find Buena Vista so I used my smartphone's GPS to plot the fastest route.

My phone rang as I pulled to the curb behind J.V.'s Camry.

"She's out of her car and walking down the driveway at the end of the street. I can't see the house from here. You want me to follow?"

"No, I'll go. You can head on home."

"I'll stick around in case you need me."

I tucked the Ruger into the holster at the small of my back and stuffed my hair up under the baseball cap, for all the good it would do. If I came face to face with Nina, even in the dark, I was sure she would recognize me.

J.V. had his window rolled down and was puffing on a rum scented cigar. I could smell it as I jogged past the Camry.

I slowed to a walk when I reached the long driveway. I had expected a gate, but there wasn't one. I walked about thirty yards before the ranch-style house came into view. Lights were on in a couple of the front rooms and an overhead light illuminated the front porch. The door was closed. This would be a really good time to have night vision goggles. Nina could be hiding anywhere on the grounds and I wouldn't see her until she was on top of me.

I drew the Ruger and held it, muzzle down, at my side. I moved off the driveway as I approached the house, stopping about ten yards from the front door and concealing myself behind a tree.

Only moments passed before the door opened and Nina stepped outside. She closed the door behind her and took off a pair of latex gloves while surveying her surroundings. I had a choice to make. Confront Nina, or check to see if anyone in the house was bleeding to death. If Nina was as efficient tonight as she had been in the past, the EMTs would never arrive in time.

She started walking down the driveway. When she was about four yards away I stepped out from behind my tree.

"Nina," I said. "This has got to stop."

She whirled in my direction and her hand dove into her purse. I raised the Ruger.

"Hands where I can see them," I said.

If I kept taking homicide cases I was going to have to invest in a Kevlar vest and a pair of cuffs.

"How do you know my name?" she asked. Her right hand was still inside her purse.

"Hands where I can see them," I repeated.

"I don't have much money," she said. "But you can have all I've got."

"I'm not here to rob you, you idiot. I'm here to stop you, now get your fucking hand out of your purse!"

I was moving slowly toward her and saw recognition suddenly ignite her features.

"Nicoli? What are you doing here?"

"I work for Gloria Freedman's son. You remember, the woman you killed at Mervyn's? Now for the last time take your hand out of your purse or I swear to God I'll shoot."

"You wouldn't do that. I'm not armed."

"Believe me, I will. It's over, Nina."

She removed her hand from her shoulder bag and took a step toward me.

"Hands on your head," I said, thinking I needed to get that purse, and the knife I knew it concealed, away from her.

Nina held her hands out in front of her. Not very good at following directions.

"Put your fucking hands on top of your head, *now*!" I barked.

My heart was pounding and I was sweating in spite of the cool weather.

I was only a few yards away now, wanting the purse, but afraid of getting in close enough to grab it. Nina raised her hands to shoulder height keeping them out in front of her.

"Drop the purse!"

She lifted the shoulder strap with her left hand and held the purse out to me. As I reflexively reached for the bag she let it fall and lunged at me. I heard a crackling sound and felt the searing burn as every one of my muscles contracted. Then I felt myself slide away.

C⊙ ⊙)

From somewhere in the darkness I heard a voice calling my name. I struggled through the swamp of unconsciousness and forced my eyes open. J.V. was bending over me, holding my hand, a look of panic on his face.

"What happened?" I asked, the words thick in my mouth.

"I'm not sure. I saw Nina drive away and decided I'd better check on you. Found you lying here on the ground."

"Oh, shit," I mumbled. "Taser. She hit me with a taser." I tried to sit up, but my muscles wouldn't cooperate. I spotted my Ruger lying beside me and was grateful Nina hadn't taken it. It had been my first handgun and had some sentimental value.

"You want me to call an ambulance?" J.V. asked.

"Not for me, but you might want to see if anyone in the house needs one."

"You sure you're okay?"

"No, but I will be in a minute. Give me your cigar. I need nicotine."

J.V. handed me the cigar and moved off toward the house. I rolled onto my side so I could watch. He approached the front door, pressed the doorbell, and waited. I puffed on the cigar and finally managed to sit up. When no one answered, J.V. reached for the knob and pushed the door open. He stood there for a full minute, not moving, then he pulled the door closed again and turned to face me. He shook his head. I knew that headshake. It was the same headshake a surgeon gave family members when someone didn't make it to the recovery room.

CHAPTER 37

I WAS CONCERNED ABOUT J.V. MISSING
his flight home and how this whole mess
might affect the adoption process, so I
suggested he just drive away. I volunteered
to tell the responding officers that Nina had
hit me with a taser, and when I regained
consciousness I checked the house and
found the body. J.V. insisted two witnesses
were better than one, and besides, his prints
were on the doorknob. He had a point.

J.V. called 911, and I retrieved my phone
from my car and called Bill. I told him about
the murder and gave him an abbreviated
version of what I had been doing the last
two days.

He was silent for a long moment before
asking if I was all right, and it shook me.

"I'm fine," I said.

"I'll be there as soon as possible." He disconnected without saying anything further. I could feel the heat of his anger.

The Los Altos police department showed up in force—three patrol cars and a pair of plainclothes detectives. The uniforms secured the scene and the detectives escorted me and J.V. off the property and questioned us separately.

Ten minutes into the questioning I saw Bill's unmarked car approaching, followed closely by the coroner's van.

Bill waited until I was finished talking with Detective Morris, a tall, slender, dark-haired man in his forties, then he stepped in and introduced himself. Morris shook his hand and took notes as Bill told him about the sex registrants who had recently been murdered in Redwood City, Sunnyvale, and San Mateo. He mentioned the IA investigation currently underway in Redwood City. He and Morris exchanged business cards. Morris said I was free to go and moved off toward the house. J.V. joined me and Bill a moment later, nodding his head grimly, but saying nothing.

Bill asked if I was okay to drive and I said, once again, that I was fine. But I wasn't fine. I was okay physically, but he hadn't

touched me since arriving at the scene and
I was afraid I'd damaged our relationship
beyond repair.

"I'm going to stay here for a while," Bill
said, and stalked away.

I walked J.V. to his car and asked him if
they had requested that he remain available
for further questioning.

"They said I can go back to Seattle
tomorrow, but they might be calling me
with additional questions. I gave them all
my phone numbers. What are you going to
tell Scott?"

I hadn't thought about that. Nina had yet
to be apprehended and all I had proof of was
that she had killed Jensen. In fact, I hadn't
seen her do that, so there was a chance, with
a good attorney, that she'd get off.

"I don't know," I said. "I'd like to tell
him everything, but what if Nina gets away
with it? What would you do?"

"I guess I'd wait a bit."

"That's what I'll do then."

I hugged J.V. for a long time before
he got in his car. I needed the warmth of
physical contact with someone I cared
about, and didn't expect I'd be getting any
from Bill in the near future.

I passed Bill's unmarked car as I walked

to my Bimmer and saw Buddy peering out through the windshield. His tail was wagging slowly, as though he was happy to see me but uncertain about the situation. I opened the car door and hooked him to the leash Bill had left in the back seat, then managed to get Bill's attention with a wave, pointing to Buddy, so he wouldn't worry that the boy had been kidnapped.

As soon as I was in my car I looked at the surveillance schedule and called Lily at home.

"Hi, Nikki," she said. "That house in Atherton was on the news tonight. Anthony Costa's body was found by his mother who was visiting from Fort Lauderdale. Where's Nina?"

"I have no idea. That's why I'm calling. Surveillance is off for the time being. She killed a man in Los Altos tonight. I confronted her when she came out of his house and she hit me with a taser. The police are here. Nina's probably gone home to pack a few things before skipping town."

"Should I go to her house?"

"Too dangerous. She's on the run now. I gave the Los Altos Detectives her address."

"I can follow her from a distance."

"No, Lily. It's too dangerous. Stay home, please."

CHAPTER 38

Ⓝ INA MADE IT TO *BURLINGAME* in twenty-
five minutes. She knew she had a little
time before Nicoli regained consciousness and
the ability to walk. She'd hastily searched the
PI's pockets for a cell phone, but hadn't found
one. That meant she'd have to crawl back to
her car before she could call the police.

She had seriously considered taking Nicoli's
gun, but where she was going she wouldn't be
able to conceal it. She'd thought about killing
Nicoli, but still carried the weight of killing
that woman at Mervyn's. Nicoli had called
her Gloria and said she was working for the
woman's son—the boy Nina had been trying
to save.

She replayed the events of the evening as
she shoved clothes into a duffle bag. She had
worn the blonde wig, hoping it would make

her look non-threatening, and the red dress in case there was blood. The disguise had worked like a charm. Jensen had checked her out through the peephole and opened the door without hesitation. She had asked to use his phone, claiming to have car trouble, and he'd welcomed her into his home. As he turned his back to close the door she'd hit him with the taser, and when he went down she'd jammed the knife into his heart. She took a moment to put on latex gloves so she wouldn't leave her prints on the doorknob on her way out. Everything had gone like clockwork. How the fuck had Nicoli known where she would be?

When she had packed everything she could carry, Nina took a last look around. She felt sad about leaving her little house. It was the first place she had ever felt safe, the only place she'd ever felt at home.

Before stepping outside Nina peered through a crack in the drapes. The white van was parked on her street again. She'd seen it three times in the last week. Each time the woman had a different hair color, but it was the same van.

Nina dug a pair of binoculars out of her duffle and trained them on the driver's side window. Tonight the occupant was a redhead and she was looking in Nina's direction.

She quickly ducked behind the curtains as realization struck. The woman in the van worked for Nicoli Hunter.

Nina placed the duffle and her purse next to the back door, withdrew the switchblade from her pocket, and stepped outside.

CHAPTER 39

I T WAS GOOD TO HAVE company on the drive home. Even if I had permanently screwed things up with Bill, at least I had Buddy.

By the time I arrived at the marina the adrenaline had worn off and I was trembling with fight-or-flight withdrawal. I walked Buddy around the grounds long enough for him to water some bushes, then we went to my office.

I locked the door behind me. I didn't think Nina would come after me, but I was in the phone book and there was no sense taking chances.

I took the Jose Cuervo out of my Pendaflex drawer and poured myself a shot. I took a sip of the tequila, shuddered, and called Jim Sutherland. I spent the next twenty minutes telling my story to Jim and then to Elizabeth who said she would call Jack. By the time I'd finished I was drained, but I had a nice buzz going from the tequila.

I was getting ready to leave when my cell phone rang.

"Nikki, it's Lily. Don't get mad, but I decided to check Nina's house to see if she was there."

"Oh for *Christ's* sake, Lily. What happened? Are you okay?"

"I'm fine, but she got away from me. The bitch slashed my tire. She must have snuck up behind the van. I was watching the house and I didn't see her come out. I guess she has a back door. Anyway, about ten minutes after I got here she came out the front carrying a duffle bag, got in her car, and drove away. I tried to follow her. That's when I realized I had a flat. I have to wait for Triple A to come and change the tire. I'm sorry, Nikki. I guess I blew it."

"You didn't blow anything, honey. I'm just glad you're all right."

I kicked myself for endangering my friends, thinking what else Nina might have slashed if she'd felt cornered.

I locked up the office and Buddy and I walked down to the boat. He leaped down

the companionway steps and made a beeline
for the stateroom. I followed him into the
doorway and froze.

Bill's guitar case, laptop computer, and
an open garment bag were on the bunk, and
he was packing the set of work clothes he
kept in my hanging locker.

"You're leaving?" I said in a hoarse
whisper. I had expected an argument, but I
hadn't braced myself for this.

"I think we both need some space," he
said. His voice was cold and he wasn't looking at me. Buddy prodded his thigh, trying
to get his attention, and he gently stroked
the dog's head.

"Can we talk about this before you go?
I'd like a chance to explain my point of view."

That stopped him. He turned and looked
me in the eye, and I almost took a step back.
Bill rarely got this angry, but when he did it
was scary.

"Your point of view doesn't enter into
it," he said. "You made me a promise, Nikki.
You broke your word."

"I promised not to *bother* Nina. I didn't
promise not to watch her. Is this all it takes
to drive you away?" I felt heat behind my
eyes and fought it back with my own anger.
"I was doing my job, God damn it!"

The line of his mouth hardened. "Clearly your job is more important to you than our relationship."

"That's not fair. I would never say that to you."

"I would never break a promise without talking to you about it first. Tell me something, all the late night bar surveys you've been doing, were you actually following Nina? How many lies have you told me, Nikki?"

"I've lost count. She's the fucking killer! Doesn't that make any difference to you?"

"Of course it does, but it has nothing to do with the fact that you've been lying to me."

"I *hated* lying to you, but you've got a stick up your ass when it comes to the people you work with. You wouldn't even listen to me when I told you I thought Nina might be the killer, and I have a nine-year-old client who needs to know why his mom was murdered."

"What about what I need?"

"Maybe your expectations aren't realistic."

Buddy was lying on the floor between us, his head on his forepaws, his eyes shifting back and forth, depending on who was speaking. When the conversation stopped and Bill zipped the bag closed, Buddy stood up next to me, blocking the stateroom doorway, his tail between his legs.

Bill swung the laptop case over his shoulder and hoisted the bag and the guitar case. Buddy and I did not move out of his way.

"So this is it?" I asked.

"I don't know. I need some time to think."

I was absolutely *not* begging him to stay. I'd been through a lot tonight, and the man in my life should want to comfort me.

"J.V. is still at your house, you know. His flight leaves early tomorrow morning."

"I can sleep on the couch." His eyes softened a little. "I'll call you," he said.

I grabbed Buddy's collar to keep him from following Bill and stepped back into the galley. Bill struggled to fit through the hatch with all of his luggage. He closed the hatch behind him and I heard him move out of the pilothouse, then felt the boat sway as he stepped onto the dock.

I fought the urge to go after him. I didn't know what I would say. *"I'm sorry"?* But I *wasn't* sorry. I had done what needed to be done. Of course, I was sorry about all

the lying and promise breaking, but he knew
that, right? I'd told him I hated lying to him.

I collapsed onto the galley settee and let
the tears come.

CHAPTER 40

BUDDY SLEPT ON THE BED that night. Okay, Buddy sleeps on the bed every night. I didn't get any rest, but his proximity was comforting.

At 9:00 a.m. I threw back the covers and sat up. Buddy gazed at me, his tail thumping, and leaned in close enough to lick my nose. I figured that was puppy-speak for "I need a walk."

I pulled on my sweats and picked up his leash. That elicited a happy chuff before he climbed the steps and opened the hatch. I followed him up into the pilothouse. When we stepped onto the dock I hooked the leash to his collar before we started walking.

After making the rounds of all Buddy's favorite trees and shrubs we walked back down to the boat and I started a pot of coffee.

I showered while the coffee was brewing. When I was dry and dressed I poured a mug and turned on the news.

CNN had a breaking story about a man who had been killed in the Woodside Hills over the weekend. His housekeeper had found him when she arrived for work this morning. I glanced at the screen and recognized the house on Ranch Road. It was the house I'd followed Nina to on Friday night.

I reluctantly picked up the phone and called Bill. I dialed his office number, hoping I'd get voicemail because I wasn't ready for any fresh pain, but he picked up.

"I assume you've heard about the murder in the Woodside Hills?" I began.

"Giordano? Yeah, I've heard about it. Why?"

"I followed Nina to that house on Friday night. Jim Sutherland can corroborate. He relieved me at two a.m., and he was there when she came out of the house." Silence. I waited a beat. "Bill?"

"Yeah. I'm taking notes."

"Has Nina been picked up yet?"

"Not that I know of. Los Altos PD has an APB out on her. She wasn't at her house by the time they got there."

"You want me to come in and make a statement?"

"Woodside Hills is handled by the San Mateo County Sheriff's Department. Let me give them a call and get back to you."

"Okay."

He hung up without another word. Even though he hadn't said anything unkind, I felt stung by the hang up and by his tone of voice.

I called Jim to let him know about Giordano. He turned on the TV in his office and watched the news story as we spoke.

"This is good," he said. "Now they can get her for at least two homicides."

"If they can catch her."

After talking to Jim, I called Elizabeth. I filled her in on what was happening with Nina and then I told her Bill had gone home angry last night.

"Oh, honey. Are you okay?"

"No. I could use a visit. You feel like coming over for dinner?"

"I think I can work that into my schedule. What should I bring?"

"Bring the wine. I'll make a kitchen sink salad."

"Yum. See you at six."

Feeling relieved that someone still loved

me, I finished my coffee and ate some yogurt while making a shopping list. Kitchen sink salad is my own recipe and includes organic lettuce, cashews, sunflower seeds, grated mozzarella, diced chicken, avocado, mushrooms, cucumber, radishes, artichoke hearts, hearts of palm, and the dressing of your choice. I like shitake mushroom vinaigrette but Buddy prefers ranch.

I was just tucking the list into my purse when J.V. called.

"I hate to say I told you so," he began.

"Hi, J.V. How was your flight?"

"Uneventful, which is how I like it. That man of yours was mighty pissed when he got home last night."

"I'm aware of that."

"You should have told him sooner."

"Maybe."

"He loves you, you know. Men don't get that angry with women they don't care about."

"What's your point?"

"It's not too late to fix this, Nicoli. But you may need to apologize."

"I'll think about it."

"You do that."

"Thanks for calling, J.V."

"Uh huh." And he hung up.

I hate being told what to do.

That afternoon I took Buddy to two restaurants and a bar, leaving him in the car of course, but treating him to leftover poached salmon and sirloin burger. When I was done with the surveys I went to the Whole Foods grocery on Jefferson and picked up a bag of Buddy's organic kibble along with the monster salad ingredients.

Bill called my cell while I was shopping and gave me the names of the detectives handling the Giordano investigation for the Sheriff's department. I said I would call them when I got home and promised to convey the contact information to Jim Sutherland.

After unloading the groceries, I called Jim and gave him the detectives' names and phone numbers. I called the Sheriff's Department and got voicemail for Detective Harding. I left a message stating who I was and why I was calling, leaving all three of my numbers. Then I set to work creating a culinary masterpiece. The salad bowl weighed at least five pounds by the time I was finished. I squirted some lemon juice on the avocados so they wouldn't brown, covered the bowl with Saran wrap, and muscled it into the fridge.

◯◯ ◯◯

Elizabeth knocked on one of the port lights a few minutes after six and Buddy responded with a big-dog bark before he realized it was one of his favorite people who had startled him.

Elizabeth had brought two bottles of 2005 Aldo Conterno Barolo Bussia Soprano. I foresaw a headache in my future. She set the wine on my galley counter and turned to look at me.

"I'm so sorry, honey," she sighed.

She wrapped her arms around me and I felt a tear slide down my face. "Oh, crap," I muttered.

Elizabeth uncorked one of the bottles and I produced a pair of Plexiglas wine goblets. They weren't elegant, but glassware doesn't survive long on a sailboat.

"To new beginnings," she toasted.

I took a sip of the wine. It was extraordinary. I'm not a connoisseur, but the fragrance reminded me of plums and currants, and there was a wonderful coffee-like aftertaste.

I served up the salad and Elizabeth groaned appreciatively when she took her first bite.

"Has Jack said anything to you

about being his best man?" she asked after swallowing.

"Not yet."

"He's probably waiting for the right moment. You know how important timing is to Jack. Why don't you come over to his house for dinner on Friday?"

"Sounds good."

"So what's happening with Nina?"

"Did Lily tell you she slashed one of the van's tires last night?"

"She called me this morning."

"As far as I know Nina hasn't been apprehended yet. You know that house in the hills I tailed her to on Friday night?"

"Yes. Jack and I followed her home from there, remember?"

"That's right. Well, the guy who lived there was found dead this morning."

"Holy shit."

"You know about the dead guy in Atherton, and the one in Noe Valley, right?"

"Lily told me."

"So, by my count, she's killed nine people, that we know of."

"Have you said anything to Scott?"

"No. I think I'll wait until she's in custody."

"What if she isn't arrested? What if she's arrested but not convicted?"

"I'm not thinking that far ahead." Okay, I *was* thinking that far ahead, but I couldn't protect Scott from all the injustice in the world. If Nina was arrested and not convicted, J.V. would have be the one to help him deal with it.

We'd finished most of the salad and all of one bottle of wine when Elizabeth said, "What are you going to do about Bill?"

I uncorked the second bottle and poured.

"I'm going to apologize, if he gives me a chance."

"Wow, I'm impressed. You love him, don't you?"

"I guess I do. I've had this big empty place in the center of my chest since he left last night. I honestly don't know how I could have done anything differently, but I think I need to apologize for lying to him."

"Good for you. When?"

"I don't know. He needs some time to cool off."

"If you wait, you might lose your nerve."

"Yeah, but I don't want to do it over the phone and I can't invite him over when he's this pissed off."

"Why don't you just show up at his house?"

"Without an invitation?"

"Absolutely. And bring a gift."

"What kind of a gift?"

"I don't know. What does he like?"

"He likes guns and guitars. Maybe I'll buy him some of those fancy guitar strings he uses. I think they're called Elixir. But, what if he doesn't invite me in?"

"You can give him the strings and apologize on the front porch. Either way you've done what you set out to do."

"Elizabeth, I'm scared," I whispered.

"I know honey. Love is the most frightening thing in the world for a control freak."

"Excuse me? I am *not* a control freak."

"Whatever you say. Have some more wine."

We finished the second bottle, and after Elizabeth left I took two buffered aspirin in anticipation of the hangover to come.

CHAPTER 41

C

A FTER SLASHING THE VAN'S TIRE *Nina had driven to SFO, parked her car in the long-term lot, and switched license plates with an older model Volvo.*

She'd hiked to the international terminal, located a ladies' restroom, and waited.

A little after 4:00 a.m., when restroom traffic was light, a woman Nina's approximate height and weight entered. There was no one else in the room at that time, so she stunned the woman with her taser and dragged her, and her carry-on bag, into the handicapped stall.

Nina rifled the woman's purse, locating her passport, driver's license, and boarding pass. She checked the photos and thought the resemblance was close enough. The woman had long hair, but her features were nondescript, as were Nina's. She removed the woman's diamond wedding set and put it on her left hand, hoping there wasn't a husband waiting outside.

She gagged the woman with the scarf she had been wearing and tied her hands and feet with pantyhose she found in the bag, then dumped out the suitcase and emptied the contents of her duffle into the elegant carry-on. She stuffed her own purse into the suitcase and draped the woman's Armani bag over her shoulder. At the last minute she remembered the rigorous security checkpoints and removed the switchblade and taser from her pockets, gave the woman a second jolt with the taser, and reluctantly buried her weapons in the trash.

CHAPTER 42

O N TUESDAY I WOKE WITH the anticipated headache. I took two more aspirin and started the coffee brewing before climbing into the shower. Between the aspirin and the hot water I began to feel almost human, but opted to skip the gym in favor of a big breakfast. I scrambled three eggs and threw in some precooked turkey sausage, which I shared with Buddy.

After breakfast we took a walk around the marina and then opened the office.

I had a voicemail message from Detective Harding asking me to call him back and schedule an interview. There was also a message from J.V. asking how I was doing today and what was happening with Nina.

I called J.V. first.

"Trusty and Associates."

"Hi, J.V."

"Hello, young lady. What's happening with our case?"

"Still no arrest, as far as I know."

"That's a shame."

"What's on your calendar this week?"

"Scott has his interview tomorrow. He's nervous."

"I think he has a problem with authority figures."

"Poor kid. I told him to be himself and tell the truth and everything would be fine, but I guess I'm a little nervous too."

"There's no reason in the world they wouldn't let you adopt him, J.V. You're the best thing that's ever happened to Scott."

"Thank you, Nicoli. That means a lot to me. Listen, I've been thinking about your fee."

"What fee?"

"For Scott's case."

"That's already been paid. Scott gave me some change when we signed the contract."

"I know you have expenses. And what about all your friends who've been helping out?"

"They don't expect anything."

"I'd like to pay you your normal rate for your time and theirs."

"That's not necessary."

"Damn it, I know it's not necessary. That's the whole point!"

"Don't get excited. Why don't we compromise? I'll work up a bill for half my usual rate."

"I guess that'd be okay. What's happening with you and Bill?"

"I'm going over to his house tonight to apologize."

"Good luck, kiddo. Keep me posted if anything changes."

"I will."

I called Harding next and made an appointment for 1:30 that afternoon.

After typing and e-mailing reports on all my recent surveys, Buddy and I drove to Gryphon Stringed Instruments in Palo Alto, and I purchased two sets of Elixir guitar strings. They didn't gift wrap, so we stopped at the CVS Pharmacy at Sequoia Station for a gift box, wrapping paper, and ribbon.

Back at the office I carefully wrapped the package, feeling apprehensive about showing up unannounced to make my apology.

At 1:15 Buddy and I drove to the San Mateo County Sheriff's office, which is conveniently located at the Government Center in Redwood City. It's convenient because it's only about a mile from the marina. I found a parking space under a tree. Even though the weather was cool, the sun was out and I didn't want Buddy to roast.

I opened the sunroof, rolled up the windows enough so Buddy couldn't escape, and locked the car doors. I took my Ruger and the defense spray out of my purse and locked them in the trunk. I marched up to the security guards and presented my purse, which went through the scanner. I removed the miniature defense spray canister from my keychain and handed it over.

Once I'd passed through security I stepped into the lobby and asked the deputy at the front desk to let Detective Harding know I was waiting. He made a call and then directed me to the third floor where I repeated this process with a uniformed receptionist. She told me to have a seat.

I paced around the reception area until Harding came out to get me, which was approximately seven minutes and forty-one seconds after I arrived, but who's counting. He was about five-nine and stocky, with dark hair receding toward the center of his scalp, a mustache that needed to be trimmed, and brown eyes that matched his name. He was dressed in a white shirt with the sleeves rolled up to his elbows and a pair of brown, synthetic fiber slacks. He did not offer to shake my hand.

Harding escorted me into the detective bureau and walked me to his cube, rather than to an interview room, which I took as a good sign. He sat down behind his desk and pointed to the visitor's chair. I planted myself in the chair and waited some more while he dug through the files on his desk. When he found the folder he was looking for he opened it, took out some pieces of note paper, read them, then put them back in the folder and closed it.

He finally looked at me. "I understand you have a statement to make regarding Giordano's killing."

"How much did Detective Anderson already tell you?" I asked, not wishing to spend any more time with Harding than necessary.

"Why don't you assume he hasn't told me anything and start from the beginning?"

I stifled a sigh. "I was hired to investigate the murder of Gloria Freedman. That investigation connected to several sex registrant killings, the commonality being the weapon and the fact that it was coated with garlic. It occurred to me that the killer must have unlimited access to the sex registrant data-base, among other things, and that led me to suspect the killer worked for the county."

Harding's eyes narrowed when I said that, but I forged on.

"I asked Detective Anderson to take me on a tour of the RCPD at a time when swing shift employees would be working, because all of the killings at that point had taken place during the day, many of them on weekdays. Among the employees he introduced me to was Nina Jezek, the swing shift data entry clerk in records. This next part might be hard for you to understand, but when I shook Jezek's hand I got a feeling similar to an electric shock. There's no other way to describe it. Based on that feeling I decided to tail her for a couple of days. I asked some friends to help me out. That's how Jim Sutherland got involved. Have you spoken with him yet?"

"Mister Sutherland came in and gave his statement this morning."

"So you already know all of this."

"Please continue."

"A few minutes after midnight on Saturday morning I followed Jezek from the RCPD to the Village Pub, where she met a man who turned out to be Giordano.

They talked at the bar for a few minutes and then she followed him to a house on Ranch Road in the Woodside Hills. I saw her go into the house and she was still inside at approximately 2:00 a.m., when Jim Sutherland relieved me."

"What was she wearing?" he asked.

"A white dress and high-heeled sandals."

"And her vehicle?"

"Black Toyota Celica."

"Anything else you'd like to add to your statement?"

I looked around for the tape recorder. I didn't see one and he hadn't been taking notes.

"Are you taping this?" I asked.

"I have an excellent memory."

"I don't mind if you're taping it," I said. "I'm just curious. I don't see a tape recorder anywhere."

"Do you want to add anything to your statement?" he asked again.

"Just that Jezek is also being sought in connection with a homicide that took place in San Francisco Saturday night and one that took place in Atherton on Sunday around noon, as well as the most recent murder in Los Altos."

"Okay. Thank you for coming in."

He extended his hand and I shook it. His palm was dry and slightly calloused, his grip was firm but not overbearing, and touching him did not give me a warm feeling.

Buddy was happy to see me. I walked him around the outside of the complex and let him pee on several bushes before we got back in the car.

I rolled the windows all the way down, lit a cigarette, and considered the interview process. If Harding had been taping our conversation he had a legal obligation to say so. When I'd asked him if he was taping it, he had refused to answer. What the hell was that about? And why interview me at his desk instead of in an interview room where everything would automatically be videotaped? My best guess was that he was trying to put me at ease by talking to me at his desk, hoping I would offer more information. Regardless, the guy was a creep.

I replayed the whole conversation in my head as we drove back to the marina.

Buddy and I walked down to the boat and had lunch, then I took a nap, still trying to recover from the previous night's indulgence.

I woke up after 5:00, showered, primped, and drank some coffee before selecting my outfit for the apology extravaganza. I decided on jeans and a sweater, under which I wore my black lace Natori bra and panties.

At 6:30 Buddy and I walked up to the parking lot. He hopped into the back of the Bimmer and we drove to Bill's house.

The Mustang was parked in the driveway when we arrived. There was a bronze Lexus SUV parked on the street in front of the house, but that wasn't unusual. Madison Avenue is always crowded with cars. I pulled into the driveway behind Bill's Mustang.

Hooking Buddy's leash to his collar, I slung my purse over my shoulder, and collected the gift box. My heart was pounding and I was so nervous I was afraid the power of speech might elude me. Buddy and I stepped onto the porch and I rang the doorbell.

I could hear people talking inside the house. Was that a woman's voice? I was pondering what that might mean when the door opened and I was greeted by a tall blonde with large Bambi eyes and a supermodel figure draped in a fuchsia wrap dress. She had a cocktail in her hand.

"Hello," she said warmly. "You must be Nicoli."

She reached out and stroked Buddy's silky head and the traitor wagged his tail.

I was, as I had feared, speechless.

"Who is it, Annie?" Bill called from somewhere in the house.

"I think it's Nicoli," she responded.

I thrust the guitar strings at her and turned on my heel. Buddy resisted my attempts to get him back into the car. Bill was nearby and he liked the nice lady in the pink dress. I tugged on his leash and swore at him.

"Nikki?"

I looked over my shoulder and saw Bill standing on the porch. He was holding a dishtowel in one hand and the gift box in the other. Annie stood behind him, looking amused. He looked bewildered and angry.

"Where are you going?" he growled.

"I came over to apologize," I hissed through my teeth, "for lying to you, you son of a bitch. I'm sorry I lied to you, and you can go straight to hell!"

I finally picked Buddy up and heaved him into the backseat. I jumped in the car, slammed the door, cranked the engine, and almost ran over Bill's foot trying to get out of the driveway.

"Wait a minute!" he shouted. "Just a God damned minute!"

I had to escape. My eyes were filling

with tears and the last thing I needed was for Bill to know how hurt I was that he hadn't even waited two days before moving on. *Unbelievable.* I finally find a man I *might* want to spend my life with, we have one fight, and he's with another woman before I can even get my act together enough to apologize. I am such a fool!

I felt a breach in the center of my chest. Love sucks. This was it for me. I was done. Men weren't worth the trouble, except that Bill *had* been worth the trouble. Bill was great, the fucking jerk.

I made it about a block before my cell phone rang. I stopped at an intersection and checked the display. It was Bill. I turned the phone off and threw it at my purse.

CHAPTER 43

NINA JEZEK, OR ELLEN JENKINS as she was now calling herself, stopped in Paris only long enough to book a flight to Amsterdam. She had enough cash to pay for the ticket and a couple of nights in a hotel once she reached her destination. When she landed in Amsterdam she would call her bank and have them wire her some money. Then she would change identities again. That shouldn't be too hard in a place like Amsterdam.

The flight was jarring. Her seat was in coach where the passengers were jammed together like sardines. Nina didn't like being close to other people. She didn't like being touched or jostled, but she tolerated it because she was on a mission.

Once she had established her new identity and taken care of Giordano's suppliers in

Europe, Asia, and South America, she would go back to the states and finish off his remaining clients. One of his suppliers was in Tijuana. Maybe she'd have some plastic surgery done while she was there. She wondered if they could alter her fingerprints.

From the Schiphol airport she took a taxi to Hotel Sofitel. They had a vacant suite and were happy to accept her American dollars.

Nina followed the bellman to the elevator, not bothering to take in her opulent surroundings. She retrieved her suitcase from him at the door to the suite and gave him an appropriate tip, not wanting to stand out in his mind as being either too generous or too stingy.

She put out the 'Do Not Disturb' sign before locking herself in for the night. She'd been in the air for more hours than she could remember. Her stomach was upset from the airplane food, and she was exhausted.

Nina took a long hot shower, wrapped herself in the complimentary bathrobe, and fell into a restless sleep.

CHAPTER 44

I DROVE BACK TO THE MARINA fighting to see through a film of tears. Buddy was licking my ear, knowing something was wrong and wanting to make it better.

I parked, not quite between the lines, in the boat owner's lot, grabbed my purse and Buddy's leash, and slipped on my sunglasses so my neighbors wouldn't stop me to ask what was wrong. We managed to make it to the boat without an encounter.

I dug around under the sink until I found the Jameson's, took a tumbler from the shelf, filled the glass three quarters of the way with Guinness Stout, and topped it off with a shot of the whiskey. I stirred it with my finger and took a sip. Now here was a hangover remedy. Of course the hangover would only be gone until the next morning, but at the moment I didn't care.

I took another sip, lit a cigarette, and looked at my cell phone. I had one message. I didn't want to hear the message. The message was from Bill, who had a new woman in his life two days after storming out on me.

I picked up my landline and called Elizabeth.

"Help," I said, when she answered.

"What happened?"

"I went to his house with two sets of Elixir guitar strings, which are not cheap by the way. I even gift-wrapped them, and he was with... he was with... another *woman!*"

"Who was she?" she asked.

"How the fuck do *I* know? She was *beautiful*, that's who she was. She was my fucking *replacement*!"

"Honey, I hate to interrupt your wallowing, but how do you know that? Did you ask?"

"Of *course* not! I wasn't going to stick around and let them rub it in my face!"

"So you don't know who she was. She could be a friend. She could be his neighbor. Tell me exactly what happened."

I told her every agonizing detail and

when I was finished she said, "Have you listened to the voicemail message yet?"

"No. I don't want to hear anything he has to say."

"I love you, Nikki, but you're being childish. Listen to the message and hold your cell up to the receiver so I can hear it too."

"Elizabeth…"

"Stop being stubborn and play the message. You know you're dying to hear it."

"Am not!" I snapped.

I keyed in the voicemail code and held the cell up to my ear with the mouthpiece of my handset close enough so Elizabeth could hear.

"Thank you for the guitar strings," said Bill, his tone clipped. "And thank you for the apology, such as it was. If you had stuck around for a minute I would have introduced you to my *friend*, Anne. I bought the house from her and her *husband* Alex six years ago, and we got close. I needed a woman's opinion about what happened with you, so I bribed her with dinner if she would listen to my problems. For your information, she says I'm behaving like a caveman. Call me. I love you. Bitch."

I saved the message and put the cell down on the galley counter.

"See," said Elizabeth. "He loves you and she's just a friend. A *married* friend."

"Maybe."

"Nikki, sweetie, get a grip. You over-reacted. Now you have to apologize all over again."

"No way. I am never doing that again."

"Okay, you don't have to apologize. But you do have to call him."

"Maybe tomorrow."

"If you don't call him right now and call me back and tell me you patched things up, I'm not going to be able to sleep tonight. Do you really want to do that to your best friend in the world?"

"That's not fair."

"Don't make me come over there. Make the call, and call me *back*," she shouted, and hung up.

I looked at the phone, then I looked at Buddy who was lying on the floor gazing up at me with a question in his big brown eyes. He missed Bill. *I* missed Bill. I played the voicemail message again, drank half of the boilermaker, and smoked another cigarette. Then I dialed Bill's number.

Nancy Skopin

The phone rang twice before he picked up.

"Hello, Nikki."

"So Anne thinks you're behaving like a caveman, huh? What else did she say?"

"She said I put you in a position where you had to lie to me in order to do your job, and the fact that you were willing to jeopardize our relationship in order to take care of your client shows integrity."

"I think I like her."

"Yeah, she's okay."

There was an awkward silence.

"So, what happens now?" I asked.

"I don't know. You want to have dinner tomorrow night?"

"Okay. I'll cook. Sixish?"

"See you tomorrow."

I hung up the phone feeling scared and confused. Having dinner didn't mean we were getting back together. Having dinner meant we were having a date.

I called Elizabeth back and she picked up before the phone finished ringing even once.

"So?"

"I'm making him dinner tomorrow night."

"Excellent! Wait. What does that mean?"

"I don't have a clue."

338

"Relationships are hard work, Nikki. But he's worth it, right?"

"Yeah, he's worth it. I'm exhausted."

"I know, honey. Go to bed. You need a good night's sleep after the last week."

"Okay. Elizabeth?"

"Yes?"

"Thank you."

"For what?"

"For being my friend."

"Yeah. It's a dirty job, but somebody's gotta do it," she laughed, and hung up.

I finished my drink and fell into bed with Buddy curled up by my side.

CHAPTER 45

I WOKE UP FEELING SURPRISINGLY WELL on Wednesday morning. It was a sunny day, and although my head was a little fuzzy, it wasn't an unpleasant fuzziness.

I started a pot of Kona coffee and took a quick shower before turning on the TV. International news came on after the NASDAQ report. I felt a chill slither up my spine as the CNN anchor reported on a double homicide that had taken place in Amsterdam's red light district. Abel and Dorothea VanKeuren had been stabbed to death. The middle-aged couple had been suspected of trafficking in the sale and exportation of minors for the purpose of sexual exploitation. Interpol had been investigating them.

Had Nina had gone international?

I finished my coffee and brushed my teeth before calling Bill. I told him about the murders in Amsterdam and suggested he inform Interpol about the local killings, and Nina.

"You want me to bring anything to-night?" he asked.

"Um, sure, you can bring dessert."

"You never eat dessert."

"I was speaking figuratively."

I could almost hear the gears grinding. "Oh," he said with a smile in his voice. "Maybe I'll get there early and we can have dessert before dinner."

Buddy and I spent the late morning and early afternoon taking care of restaurant and bar surveys in Sunnyvale, Mountain View, and Menlo Park. We were both overfed when we got back to the marina. I walked him around the grounds before opening the office.

I checked my voicemail and e-mail, tossed my survey notes into my inbox, and started a shopping list. I didn't want anything too filling for dinner, in case there was dessert before and after, so I made a list of salad ingredients, then added wild salmon and teriyaki marinade. Bill is a big fan of carbohydrates, so I included rice on the list.

When I was satisfied that I'd provided for every dietary contingency, Buddy and I set out for the Whole Foods store on Jefferson.

After I'd packed all my groceries in the trunk of my car, I glanced at my watch. Bill wasn't due until 6:00, and it was only 3:45. I had time to go lingerie shopping.

I drove north to the Hillsdale Mall and started at Nordstrom but ended up at Forever21 where I picked up a short, red silk kimono with gold and black embroidery. My plan was to greet Bill in the kimono and nothing else.

We arrived back at the marina a little after 5:00. I loaded my purchases into a dock cart and wheeled them down to the boat. I put the salad stuff in the sink and started the salmon marinating before I showered.

I spritzed a little Must De Cartier behind my ears and in my cleavage, and put on the kimono. I climbed the steps into the pilothouse and locked the door, so Buddy couldn't let himself out when he heard Bill's car.

I was assembling salad ingredients at 5:55 when Buddy started dancing in place. When I didn't respond, he climbed the steps to the hatch and opened it, letting himself into the pilothouse, then stood staring back at me for a minute before he took the door handle between his teeth and tried to pull open it. When that didn't work he started whining.

"You can wait for him here," I said.

He looked at me over his shoulder, his ears pinned back in disapproval.

"Buddy, come," I said.

He turned away, stubborn boy.

We didn't have long to wait. I felt the boat sway and went up to unlock the door. Buddy barely let me get the door open before lunging outside to greet Bill, who tussled with the big puppy as his eyes took in my kimono and the obvious lack of undergarments.

"Hi," he said.

When Buddy felt he had been adequately loved-up, he leaped down the companionway and Bill kissed me with a lot of tongue, groping me through the kimono.

"Let's go inside," I said, not wanting to give my neighbors too much of a show.

We had dessert before dinner, and after dinner, and again in the middle of the night. We didn't talk about the future. I was afraid to broach the subject.

In the morning I got up and made him breakfast, in the kimono. Breakfast got cold while we had a repeat performance of the night before.

When he left for work I lingered over coffee, basking in the afterglow and feeling pretty good about life in general.

I showered, dressed, and walked Buddy, then unlocked the office and flipped on the TV in my kitchenette while I was making coffee. I tuned it to CNN, anxious to see if Nina had struck again, but there were no new murders being reported.

I typed up my surveys from the day before and e-mailed them off with attached invoices.

I had a couple of dinner surveys to do that night, so I called Lily to see if she felt like coming along.

"Free food?" she said. "Of *course* I'll come. What time?"

"I'll meet you at the office at 5:00."

"Okay. How should I dress?"

"We're going to Chez Jacques in Atherton and Barron's in Portola Valley, so dress up a little."

"Goodie!" Nobody likes to dress up more than Lily.

I called Elizabeth at work to tell her about my night of debauchery with Bill.

"Congratulations," she said, when I had

told her all the juicy details. "When are you seeing each other again?"

"We didn't make any plans."

"Uh huh," she murmured, waiting for the other shoe to drop.

"When you love someone they can rip your heart out," I said.

"I get it. You're afraid of letting Bill get close enough to hurt you again."

"Maybe."

"That's just stupid."

"Shut up."

"If you love him, you have to take that chance."

"Yeah, I know."

"So, what are you going to do?"

"Shit. I guess maybe I could tell him that I love him."

In the end, nothing was decided. My phone rang as soon as we ended the call. It was Bill.

"Hi, Nikki. Last night was great," he began, unceremoniously.

I held my breath and waited.

"I really flipped out when I found out you'd been lying to me," he continued.

"I noticed."

"I think we need some ground rules," he said.

"Ground rules?"

"Why don't I come over after work and we can talk about this in person."

"I'm doing two dinner surveys with Lily tonight. Can you come by around ten?"

"Sure. Hey, Nikki?"

"Yeah?"

"I love you."

Shit! "I love you, too," I muttered, against my better judgement.

At least Elizabeth would be happy. I'd taken a leap of faith, and it scared the crap out of me.

CHAPTER 46

NINA HAD NO DIFFICULTY LOCATING *a supplier of fraudulent documents in Amsterdam. She purchased three new identities, including passports, driver's licenses, and credit cards.*

On one of her walks through the red light district, while stalking the VanKeurens, she discovered a specialty shop where she purchased a make-up bag lined with lead, ideal for transporting small weapons in one's luggage. This would save her the trouble of finding a new knife in each country she intended to visit. She planned to surround the knife with tampons, in case the blank spot in her luggage aroused curiosity going through an airport security scanner. She had been unable to find a stiletto switchblade in Amsterdam, but she had found an adequate knife with a long narrow

Nancy Skopin

blade, and a vinyl sheath, which she coated with garlic oil.

Nina was ready to move on within a week. She took a taxi to the Schiphol airport and booked a flight to Changsha, China. Her ultimate destination was Guizhou, but the nearest airport was in Changsha.

She picked up an English/Tujia dictionary at the duty free shop, and began studying it while she waited for her boarding call.

CHAPTER 47

LILY AND I DINED ON excruciatingly delicious French and Spanish cuisine while discussing Nina's psychoses. We share an interest in psychology and Lily's insights have proved enlightening in the past. Her general knowledge rivals my own, but when it comes to understanding deviant behavior she leaves me in the dust.

"I think she's compulsively doing what she couldn't do for herself as a child," Lily said, "protecting the innocent from predators. She's probably projecting her own childhood persona onto the children she's trying to rescue."

While listening to Lily, I developed a clearer picture in my mind of what was motivating Nina, and I began to feel sorry for her.

Eventually the conversation turned to the predators Nina was killing.

"Genuine pedophiles are driven by an uncontrollable impulse," Lily said, "that can only be managed with medication, or castration."

"*Jeez.*"

"Yeah. Some states have begun enforcing mandatory medication, also known as chemical castration, as a condition of parole for habitual sex offenders. California is one of them, but it's difficult to enforce. There are civil rights issues, and the side effects of the drugs are unpleasant."

"Like what?"

"Well, they're designed to reduce testosterone production, but they also cause fatigue, depression, and excess salivation. Testosterone isn't what makes someone a pedophile, but it does make you hostile and horny. I've been a lot more mellow since the sex change."

By the end of the evening my mind was spinning with all the new information Lily had imparted.

Buddy and I were halfway down the dock to my boat when he stopped in his tracks and spun back toward shore. I didn't even bother trying to restrain him, I just hung onto the leash and let him drag me back up to the parking lot to meet Bill. It was just like old times, except for the fear in my gut.

When we were all onboard the boat I opened two bottles of Guinness, handed one to Bill, took a pull from my own, and said, "Tell me about these ground rules."

Bill looked at me for a long moment. "You don't lie to me about anything, ever, and I won't jump down your throat when you do something I don't approve of."

"You think you can stick to that?"

"I'll do my best."

"Okay. Deal."

I offered my hand and he shook it. Then he leaned over the galley counter and kissed me so tenderly that it made my heart ache.

"Did you talk to Interpol today?" I asked, reeling slightly from the kiss.

"I did."

"What did they say?"

"They were very interested in the details of the homicides we're attributing to Nina. I sent them copies of everything we've got on her. By the way, there was garlic oil on the knife used to kill that couple in Amsterdam."

"I *knew* it!"

We went to bed early and slept intertwined with Buddy at our feet.

Friday morning I was up at 5:00. I pulled on a pair of sweats, filled a thermal mug with coffee, and drove to the gym.

I started with an aerobics class, then used the free weights and the upper body equipment, did sit-ups and pushups, and topped it all off with the StairMaster.

I showered in the locker room and talked to my workout buddies while I was drying my hair. I was feeling optimistic about life and more than a little relieved that Nina was now Interpol's problem, and not mine.

When I got back to the boat Bill had already walked Buddy and made breakfast. Another good reason to have him around. He was domestic and I was not. I had some scrambled eggs and only one slice of bacon, with two cups of coffee. We watched CNN over breakfast, both of us waiting for any word of Nina's next victim, but there was nothing.

Bill left for work at 7:45, and I did the breakfast dishes before walking Buddy up to the office.

I had a voicemail message from J.V. saying Scott's interview had gone well and that the trial adoption period would begin next week. He was coming back this weekend for another visit, and wondered if he should book a hotel room.

I called him back and he answered after two rings.

"Trusty and Associates."

"Bill and I made up," I began. "So he'll probably be on the boat with me this weekend. Do you still have the house key?"

"Yep."

"You want me to pick you up at the airport?"

"Not necessary. I'm renting a car. Did you figure out how much I owe you?"

"I haven't had a chance. I'll do it this morning. Call me when you get here. I'd like to tell Scott about Nina and I think it might be easier for him if you're there when I do."

"Good idea."

After I hung up I decided to give Jim a call. He was out on a surveillance, so his receptionist patched me through to his cell.

"What did you think of Detective Harding?" I asked, after the usual pleasantries.

"The guy's an asshole."

"Did he tell you he was taping your interview?"

"He didn't say anything about it, so I asked. When he wouldn't answer me I insisted that it be taped. Then he showed me the hidden recorder, which had been running the whole time."

"What the hell?"

"The man has control issues."

I let Jim get back to work and pulled up my Nina surveillance schedule on the computer. I calculated the number of hours my friends and I had put in following her, added in the time we'd spent following sex offenders, and some of the time I'd spent doing research and talking with Scott. Then I divided the hours in half and multiplied them by my usual rate. It still looked like too much money so I rounded it down to three thousand dollars. I printed up an invoice and tucked it into my purse.

Around noon I remembered I was supposed to have dinner with Elizabeth and Jack. I called Bill and asked him what he was doing tonight.

"Can't wait to see me?"

"Well, yeah, but I'm having dinner with Elizabeth and Jack in Hillsborough and I was wondering if you'd be available to sit with Buddy, so they don't have to lock K.C. up."

I couldn't invite Bill to join me at dinner because Elizabeth had told me Jack planned to broach the subject of me being his best man tonight, and Jack is uncomfortable around Bill.

"What time are you leaving?"

"Six-fifteen?"

"I'll be there by six."

"Thanks."

I was smiling when we hung up.

Buddy and I walked to The Diving Pelican and ordered a Feta Salad to go, taking it back to the office so I could watch CNN while eating. Nina had killed eleven people that I knew of, and there were probably a few I didn't know about.

At four-thirty Buddy and I hiked half a mile into the wildlife refuge and back. Then we strolled down to the boat and I showered and changed into a pair of stretchy jeans in preparation for Ilsa's cooking.

Bill arrived at 5:45, and I was happy to see him. It was kind of like starting a new relationship. I hated to leave, but I did.

I was in Hillsborough by 6:20. The gate had been left open and I motored inside.

K.C. was positioned in the middle of the driveway, about ten yards from the front of the house, so I was forced to stop. I got out of the car and scratched behind his ears. He purred and rubbed his face against my legs. I picked him up and walked to the front door, which opened before I could knock. Elizabeth smiled up at me.

"You have security cameras, don't you?" I accused.

"Jack had them installed last week," she said.

I stepped inside the foyer, handed K.C. to Elizabeth, and closed the door behind me.

Jack came into the foyer carrying two glasses, one of which he offered to me. I sniffed it. It was tequila and soda, just the way I like it. Enough tequila so I can taste it, but not enough to knock me on my ass.

"Thank you, Jack." I gave him a kiss on the cheek.

We all paraded into the living room where Ilsa had set out a tray of antipasto. I picked up a wafer thin slice of prosciutto wrapped around a wedge of asiago cheese. I pinched off the end and fed it to K.C. before popping the rest into my mouth.

"What's for dinner?"

"Homemade venison sausage," Jack said. "With sauerkraut and scalloped potatoes."

"Oh my God. Ilsa makes her own sausage?"

"She's very hands-on."

"Lucky you."

"She can't wait to cater the engagement

party," Elizabeth said, and she gave Jack a gentle nudge.

"Speaking of the wedding," he began, and cleared his throat. "I have something to ask you, Nikki."

"That sounds ominous."

"I'm not very good at this kind of thing." He hesitated.

"Oh honey, just say it," Elizabeth prodded.

He said something to her in Gaelic, and she giggled.

"Will you do me the honor of being my best man at the wedding?" His face was flushed and I realized I'd never seen Jack so ill at ease. I was touched.

"I'd love to be your best man. Does that mean I get to throw you a bachelor party?"

"No strippers," Elizabeth piped up. "I mean it! No exotic dancers of any kind. "

"What about porn?"

Jack muttered something else in Gaelic and rose to refill his glass. "You want another?" he asked me.

"After dinner." I turned to Elizabeth. "Bill and I had a talk."

"And?"

"He has ground rules."

"Uh oh. What are they?"

"I don't lie to him and he doesn't climb

up my ass when I do something he doesn't like."

"Good luck with that."

Dinner was superb, as always. Over dessert of strawberries and cream, I asked Jack who he would like me to invite to the bachelor party.

"The wedding is a year and a half away," he said.

"It's never too soon to start planning."

"I don't have any male friends here."

"What about Bill?"

"You think Bill considers me his friend?"

"He likes you. He just objects to your former occupation."

"I guess you could invite Bill. But I draw the line at watching porn with you."

In fact, Jack and I had watched five videos involving girl-on-girl action last August when I was working on a case for him. Unfortunately, they were evidence, and someone was killed at the end of each home movie.

"You're not leaving me a lot of traditional bachelor party options, here," I complained. "It's supposed to be a celebration of the end of your life as a stud."

"No," said Elizabeth. "Jack will always be a stud, but now he's *my* stud."

"Maybe we should elope," Jack said.

"Not a chance," said Elizabeth. "You can have a few drinks in that nice little Irish pub on Fifth Street in San Francisco. What's it called?"

"The Chieftain?"

"That's the one. And you can smoke cigars and talk about all the girls you've loved before."

"You can't smoke in bars anymore, remember?" I said.

"I've never loved a woman before," said Jack.

"Oh, that's so sweet," Elizabeth cooed.

"Maybe I'd better leave you two alone." I collected my jacket and my purse.

"Any news on Nina?" Elizabeth asked, walking me to the door.

"I haven't heard anything since the two murders in Amsterdam. Did I tell you about those?"

"Um, *no*."

"Sorry. It was on CNN. A man and woman were killed. They were suspected of trafficking in the exportation of minors for sexual exploitation. They were both stabbed, and the knife wounds had garlic oil in them."

"Oh my *God*! She's in Amsterdam?"

"Well, she was."

I hugged Elizabeth, and before stepping outside I asked, "Should I invite Joachim to the bachelor party?"

"That's a lovely idea."

I arrived home to find Bill and Buddy asleep on the pilothouse settee. CNN was on. I glanced at the screen, grabbed the remote, and cranked up the volume.

"Hey," Bill sputtered, "When did you get home?"

I sat down beside him and silently pointed at the TV. The anchorwoman was saying something about another man who had been on Interpol's watch list. His name was Fu-han Cheung and his body had been found in an alley in Guizhou early this morning.

Bill and I looked at each other. He put his arm around me and sighed. "I'll call Interpol again tomorrow."

CHAPTER 48

A FTER THE MURDER IN GUIZHOU, Nina
had apparently killed six more people.
Those being reported included one in
Chittagong, two in Lisbon, one in Burma,
and two in Tijuana. The last reported killing
had been more than a week ago. I had
been watching CNN every day and there
had been no additional garlic murders, so
either she had changed her M.O., she was
taking a break, or she had finally given up
her vendetta.

J.V. and I had told Scott about Nina
after the Guizhou murder. He had cried,
convinced his mother's death was his fault.
We did our best to talk him out of that, but
with limited success. I'd taken him to see
my friend and therapist, Loretta Dario, a

couple of times, and he seemed lighter when I picked him up after each visit.

Scott had moved to Seattle with J.V. a few days before Christmas. Not surprisingly, his grades had improved, and J.V. told me he had two friends who came over almost every weekend.

He was also was taking guitar lessons now and feeling the normal childhood frustration about not being able to play well after only a couple of weeks. J.V. told me he practiced every day.

J.V. was taking Scott with him on low-risk, weekend surveillance jobs and said he showed a lot of potential. He'd also taken him window-shopping a couple of times, which is an old PI training tool. You take the trainee on a walk, stopping at store windows. They have thirty seconds to look at the items displayed in each window, then have to close their eyes and tell you what they saw. J.V. said Scott got all but two items on his first try. I envisioned a name change for J.V.'s agency ten years down the road—*Trusty & Son*.

Scott had called me once since moving, to thank me for everything and to tell me he'd received his mom's life insurance. He wanted to pay me. I told him the bill had already been settled by his uncle, and that he should put the money in a college fund. J.V. and I had discussed this when the insurance company cut the check.

They still had a few issues to work out. Whenever Scott misbehaved and J.V. found out about it, Scott would cower, expecting a beating. I knew J.V. would never hit a child, but Scott still needed a lot of reassurance. They were going to a family counselor once a week and things were improving. I was sure they would work everything out in time.

In mid-January Jack McGuire and Elizabeth Gaultier had their official engagement party at Jack's estate in Hillsborough. Bill, Buddy and I, Jim Sutherland, Lily, and Joachim and Ilsa Richter were the only guests. Jack and Elizabeth had written beautiful toasts to each other and I got a little choked up during this romantic ritual.

Bill tended bar at the party, and the food was set out buffet-style, because Jack insisted that Joachim and Ilsa were guests.

There were a few Buddy versus K.C. skirmishes, but no antiques were broken and after K.C. took a swipe at Buddy's nose with his razor sharp claws, Buddy decided chasing the cat wasn't such a great idea.

Since I was going to be the best man at

the wedding, still seventeen months away, I knew I would be invited to toast the future bride and groom. I'd thought long and hard about what I wanted to say. I stood near the fireplace, raised my champagne glass, consulted the index card I'd had in my pocket all evening, and said, "Slainte mhor agus a h-uile beannachd duibh. Mille failte dhuit le d'bhreid. Fad do re gun robh thu slan. Mo ran la ithean dhuit is sith. Le d'mhaitheas is le d'ni bhi fas. Meal-a-naidheachd."

Roughly translated into English that means, "Good health and every good blessing to you. A thousand welcomes to you with your wedding veil. May you be healthy all of your days. May you be blessed with long life and peace. May you grow old with goodness, and with riches. Congratulations."

Jack nearly horked champagne out of his nose at my attempt to pronounce Gaelic, and Elizabeth burst into tears.

It was a perfect evening. Watching the stolen moments of intimacy between Jack and Elizabeth almost made me reconsider my resolution never to marry again. Almost, but not quite.

Once K.C. had established his dominance over Buddy, he'd curled up in a ball at Buddy's side, cuddling up to my big dog like they were old friends. Buddy was initially nonplussed by this change in behavior, but after giving K.C. a thorough butt-sniff, he quickly settled into the new relationship.

CHAPTER 49

*O*N *FEBRUARY 25TH NINA JEZEK, currently known as Sandra Ellis, boarded an airplane at Tijuana International Airport, bound for San Francisco. She wore brown contact lenses and her shoulder length hair was honey-blonde. Her nose had been widened, her cheekbones plumped, and her fingertips permanently scarred.*

She took her seat in first class and placed her carry-on bag on the empty seat beside her. Nina had traveled to Paris, Guizhou, Chittagong, Lisbon, and Burma before stopping in Tijuana. Prior to this she had never even ventured out of the United States, and she was looking forward to going home. Returning to her beloved cottage would be impossible, of course, but at least she'd be in a country where almost everyone spoke English.

Nina knew that Interpol was hunting for her, but after all the surgical changes they would never be able to identify her. Her own mother wouldn't recognize her now.

The blood test she had finally subjected herself to revealed that she was, in fact, HIV positive, but she felt fine, just a little tired.

She glanced at her list. There were eight targets left to dispatch in California. If she managed to kill them all without getting caught maybe she could rest for a while.

~THE END~

ABOUT THE AUTHOR

Nancy Skopin is a native of California, and currently lives on the Oregon coast with her husband and their dogs.

While researching her mystery series she spent two years working for a private investigator learning the intricacies of the business. She also worked closely with a police detective who became both a consultant and a friend. She lived aboard her yacht in the San Francisco Bay Area for thirteen years, as does her central character, Nicoli Hunter.

If you'd like to be notified when new Nikki Hunter mysteries come out, email me at: NikkiMaxineHunter@gmail.com